D0827903

JUNIPER BERRY

M. P. KOZLOWSKY

Drawings by ERWIN MADRID

SCHOLASTIC INC.
New York Toronto London Auckland
Sydney Mexico City New Delhi Hong Kong

No part of this publication may be reproduced, stored in a retrieval system, or transmitted in any form or by any means, electronic, mechanical, photocopying, recording, or otherwise, without written permission of the publisher. For information regarding permission, write to HarperCollins Children's Books, a division of HarperCollins Publishers, 10 East 53rd Street, New York, NY 10022.

ISBN 978-0-545-45336-3

Text copyright © 2011 by M. P. Kozlowsky.
Illustrations copyright © 2011 by Erwin Madrid. All rights reserved.
Published by Scholastic Inc., 557 Broadway, New York, NY 10012, by arrangement with HarperCollins Children's Books, a division of HarperCollins Publishers. SCHOLASTIC and associated logos are trademarks and/or registered trademarks of Scholastic Inc.

12 11 10 9 8 7 6 5 4 3 2   12 13 14 15 16 17/0

Printed in the U.S.A.   40

First Scholastic printing, March 2012

Typography by Sarah Hoy

For Margeaux

CHAPTER 1

The house was a mansion, the lake was a pool, Kitty was a dog, and Juniper Berry was an eleven-year-old girl.

And like many eleven-year-old girls, she couldn't wait until her parents returned home from work. She sat at the top of the stairs, binoculars in hand and directed out the two-story front window, waiting to see the golden gates of her home slowly open. Tonight was Italian night and the three of them were supposed to make pizzas for dinner. This was part of their weekly schedule, only Juniper couldn't remember the last time they actually followed through with it. For a while now, everything, including her, had been neglected.

Still, she never gave up hope. One of these days her parents would come home from work and be thrilled to see her. The rest of the day and every day after would be spent in each other's company, not a minute wasted, not even a single second, just like it was years ago.

Juniper was an only child, a lonely child, mostly because her parents were adamant to keep things that way. Mr. and Mrs. Berry were very famous. They were movie stars in every sense, paid a pretty penny (plus back-end percentages) to grace the screen in summer blockbusters and year-end award fare alike. Respected, admired, even loved by peers and fans, they were unceasing fodder for the gossip columns and recognized the world over. Hence the mansion, with its gates, its seclusion.

Juniper just never thought she would be kept out as well. But indeed, everything was at a distance. The world outside might as well have been the moon or Mars or the event horizon of the blackest of black holes. She had, by now, grown accustomed to her isolation, carrying her binoculars everywhere, spying from afar, searching for what she was missing. There was a telescope on a tripod in her bedroom, a monocular of some age that she always kept tucked away in a convenient pocket, goggles for underwater adventuring, a microscope and magnifying glass for that world even smaller than hers. Discovery and exploration were her salvation; if she couldn't go out into the world, she could bring the world to her: the stars, the insects, the unsuspecting distance. Everything but her parents.

Today, however, was going to be different. She just felt it. She had it all planned out, from the moment they walked in the door until the second she fell asleep. It would go exactly like it did before they were famous.

From all the way in her past, she could still see the front door opening.

"Mommy! Daddy!" She ran to them, sprinting down the hall. Then, three feet away, she came to a screeching halt.

Mr. Berry's mouth hung oddly ajar, a sliver of saliva the bridge between two teeth. His body was twisted and awkward and his eyes were glazed over, nearly rolling back. Moaning, he lumbered right past Juniper.

"Dad?" She turned to her mother for an answer, but Mrs. Berry only shrugged, her lips strangely pursed.

Juniper turned back to her father. *What is wrong with him?* She reached out and . . .

"Ahh!" he screamed as he swung on his heels, scooping up his daughter.

Legs kicking, Juniper squealed in delight and overwhelming relief.

"Oh, I was so trying not to laugh. He's been working on it in between his auditions," Mrs. Berry explained. "You know how he gets. Has to live the lives of his characters."

"Except Juniper's zombie has more life than anything I read today." Mr. Berry laughed. "Probably why I didn't get the part." He squeezed Juniper tighter. "Is that what you were looking for, Juniper? For the zombie in your story? Did I get it right?"

Juniper nodded emphatically. "I finished writing the rest today."

Mr. Berry pointed a bony finger in the air and yelled to an imaginary assistant, "Get the kid an agent!"

"Write us a movie, Juniper," her mother said. "We'd be the first family of Hollywood!"

"I'll do it. I will."

Now, waiting for her parents, a new script tucked into her back pocket, her dog, Kitty, beside her, Juniper sat up a little straighter. They all used to get along famously, putting on their own plays in the room once kept vacant for such occasions (recently converted to a home gymnasium complete with sauna, flat-screen TVs, juice bar, hot tub, and a personal trainer). Back then, Juniper composed her short, playful scripts at a furious pace, one after the other, scene after scene, written for two.

As she directed, her parents recited lines and Juniper was wrapped in awe at how quickly they memorized them and with how much conviction each word was spoken, filling the room with thick voices, as if they breathed a fog of sound. The characters came to vivid and luscious life through their portrayals. It was as if Juniper's words now belonged to all three of them.

"Bravo! Bravo!" She cheered them on, her throat hoarse from laughter. And when the play was complete, her parents took a bow. Then they waved her onto their makeshift stage and had Juniper do the same as they applauded exuberantly. Finally, mother, father, and daughter all held hands and bowed once more in unison.

They always laughed again when they watched what they recorded each night, a fresh bowl of popcorn shared between them, their limbs lovingly overlapping. "A masterpiece," her father said every time. Juniper blushed, both then and now.

But that all could have been a lifetime ago. Juniper, still looking through her binoculars, again had to convince herself these events actually happened, that they weren't a figment of her imagination. That her parents, deep down, were still the same people they were back then.

The wait stretched from a half hour to an hour, from an hour to two hours. The sunlight was nearly extinguished, and Juniper's stomach grumbled aggressively. They had both forgotten, again. It had often come to this.

She walked to the kitchen and looked at all the cooking supplies she had neatly arranged on the counter and got started.

She made her personal pie with little fanfare. No grapefruit slices, no chocolate shavings, no crumpled potato chips. She spread the sauce and cheese joylessly. It was horrible being alone, just horrible. Of course, there was the constant stream of workers—housecleaners, gardeners, cooks, chauffeurs, handymen—and, at this moment, while Juniper was waiting for her plain cheese pizza to cook, she could hear the finishing chops of firewood by an ax man racing the coming rain. And although such employees were always about the premises, these were adults with whom she was forbidden to speak, except for her tutor, Mrs. Maybelline.

During idle moments, of which there were many, she often thought of their former house—not even a quarter of the size of this one—and how it was always bustling with aunts and uncles, grandparents, cousins, friends, the promise of school and school buses. No more. Now she didn't even have her parents.

The oven timer went off and she went about eating her meal in silence. She could barely remember the taste of those dinners past, but she knew this wasn't it.

From under the table, Kitty scratched at her leg. "You hungry?" Juniper asked, rising. "They didn't leave you anything again, did they?" Kitty wagged her tail as her bowl was filled with brown nuggets, quickly devoured.

Juniper cleaned up herself and considered retiring to her room, maybe to observe the birds and squirrels in the woods outside her window yet again. Or perhaps she would write that movie her parents always yearned for, the one that would be remembered and loved for generations to come, the movie to define their careers. Now, that would be something. But who was she kidding? She knew it wouldn't live up to their high standards. She was sure that anything she wrote would wind up in her parents' growing pile of unread scripts.

It was as she took her first step up the stairs that she heard the turn of the key in the front door.

"Mom! Dad!" She ran to them, bubbling over with excitement. *I don't care, I'll eat another pizza*, she thought. But her strides came to a sudden halt.

Her father walked in, dazed. In the shadow of the front door he looked like a stranger. Then, without any acknowledgment at all, he stepped past his daughter.

Juniper grinned. *He's going to try to scare me*, she thought. "Dad!"

But he kept walking. She turned to her mother, who promptly tossed Juniper her coat. Catching it, Juniper raced ahead to her father and reached out.

But as hard as she tugged at his sleeve, he never turned around. He just looked to the floor and spoke. "They're all amateurs. Everybody on the film. I can't believe I agreed to work with them. They're going to ruin everything. If I have to do everyone's part, then so be it."

Her mother spoke up as well. "I don't know why they cast these young girls for such demanding roles. Standards have changed, that's for sure. The poor

thing can't even pull off a British accent."

They continued talking, neither much listening to the other, and they both shrugged off Juniper, giving only a ruffle of her hair on their way past. When they came to the stairways beyond the living room, one went one way and the other went somewhere else, punctuating their departures with the slamming of doors.

There were a lot of slamming doors lately. Unfortunately, it had become normal to see her parents brooding and frustrated. By now, the days all blended together. She believed this exact moment might have happened before.

Juniper made her way up the stairs to her mother's room.

When her parents were home she often followed them around, but typically to no great satisfaction— they were lifeless. Yet, on this day, there she was again, trailing her mother through the many rooms of the mansion. The rain finally arrived and the animals Juniper so loved to watch from her window were no longer anywhere to be found, and there wasn't much else to do but discover what was troubling her mother this time. Maybe there was something Juniper could do, for once.

Mrs. Berry stormed through the house, a newspaper crumpled in one fist, a red touch phone in the other, which she was constantly dialing. She had long, thin legs with striking muscle tone. Her torso was also long and seemed to bend like warm rubber, and her fiery mane enveloped her stunning face. She had so much hair, one might not even notice how empty her eyes were.

"Juniper, dear, you go to all those websites, those gossip pages, posting boards. Have they been mentioning me? What are they saying? Where am I going, where have I been?"

"I don't read those things," Juniper muttered. And she didn't. In fact, she thought the computer was the most boring object in the house. Each time she sat before one she could swear the screen was mocking her in each flash of a page. There was information to be discovered, for sure, but none of it came to life the way it did in the backyard of her mind and home.

"Don't be silly. Of course you do. Everybody does."

"But . . . I *live* with you."

Mrs. Berry had yet to make eye contact with Juniper. Her body moved at an uncanny speed, her arms completing a multitude of tasks in seconds—she drank her coffee, popped her pills, looked in the mirror and applied some makeup, dusted some of Kitty's dog hair off her pants, popped some more pills, and ate a granola bar in three careless and rather reflexive bites. "Are they saying I'm looking older? That I need another hit? A comedy? Should I not have chosen another drama—that was your father's idea. What are they saying?"

"I don't know."

"Oh, you're useless," she snipped.

Juniper just looked down at the carpet. She couldn't help remembering, again.

"I could never live without you," her mother had once told her. "You're all I need, you and your father." Juniper thought it an odd moment to say such a nice thing. Mrs. Berry was bending over in the middle of the street, tying several packs of jumping jacks together, her longest string yet—it stretched halfway down the block. But then again, her mother always surprised her. "Get back, baby," she said in but one of her arsenal of accents. "This might get a little crazy." She lit the fuse and ran toward Juniper, ducking her head. "Get down!" And mother and daughter dove headfirst onto the grass and, heads tilted and touching, watched the skittish array of colors ping-pong across the street, slow to fade. It wasn't the Fourth of July, but it didn't matter.

Now Mrs. Berry collapsed backward onto a gargantuan and rather tacky bed, letting out a massive sigh. "I can't take it, Juniper. They always want more. More, more, more. I have only so much to give." Her lips went loose, her voice falling into a Novocain whisper. "We're trapped," she said. "Your father and me. We live two-dimensionally. Our lives aren't ours anymore." She sat up and looked at Juniper for the first time. "And you must be careful or yours will be taken, too."

Juniper crossed the room and curled next to her. Her mother's arm wrapped around her and pulled her close. For just a moment, her whole body warmed. *Please don't go*, she thought. *Don't ever leave me.*

"Mom, you can stop. You can retire," she told her.

Whatever glow was briefly in her mother's eyes immediately set. She pulled her arm back and sat straight up, peering down at her daughter. "How can you say such a thing? I'm leaving my mark on the world. Oh, you just don't get it. You never will." The words sprayed from her mouth like shrapnel, cutting Juniper deep. Mrs. Berry got up and put the phone to her ear for another listen—she was yet to place it down—then hit redial. She walked from the room without so much as a glance back at Juniper.

With Mrs. Berry whipping through the house spitting venom at workers and computer, phone and dog, Juniper ran down the long art-filled hall in search of her father. But it wasn't much of a search. She knew where he was, where he always was.

It was her favorite room of the house, just as it was her father's. She remembered the first time she stepped foot into the bilevel study occupying a large corner of the eastern wing. It was newly built, and she entered through a high-arching and heavy door on a damp yet warm morning. Covering the towering walls were thousands of books, many leather-bound, sitting on mahogany shelves, complete with a rolling ladder to reach the upper tier. They were alphabetized by author and divided and organized into categories like a public library or bookstore would do. An intricately detailed area rug—which Juniper immediately knew she would love to spread out across when streaks of sun came angling in through the massive window overhead—covered most of the herringbone-patterned floor. Matching the themes of the room were a plush leather sofa and armchair as well as an unbelievably comfortable rocking chair and cushioned ottoman in one corner, a classically ornate fireplace, expensive modern and abstract artwork, and, in the center of the room, an oversize desk craftily designed with various drawers and compartments. There was a globe that Juniper couldn't help but spin (where would her first book tour or movie premiere take her?), a shelf of acting awards, rare and signed books encased in glass—which she could not see the point of—and a collection of antique typewriters. Indeed this room had it all.

But for Juniper, the very best thing about the study was the smell. She reveled in the delightful scent wafting through the stuffy air. It was what first drew her into the room. She followed her nose down the hall, and it wasn't long before she realized it was the pages of the books that so tickled her fancy and sense of smell. She grabbed a book from off the shelves, opened the spine—hoping to hear a crack—and inhaled deeply. Then she grabbed another and another. She decided that whichever book smelled best that day, and every day after, she'd read—typically the older the better. Her father didn't mind back then, actually. He was overjoyed when he found her perusing his books that morning.

"Read as many as you want," he said, pulling her close. He liked to look in her eyes when he talked. He descended to a crouch, lovingly moving the hair out of her face. "Too much is never enough. You want to be a writer? In a way, it's similar to acting. You have to know your character's every thought. Your worlds have to collide. I have books on every career and lifestyle you can imagine. Every hobby, religion, trade. It's all here. It helps me understand everything from how my characters grew up to what type of drink they preferred and how they held it. It can do the same for you."

"That's how you became famous? That's the secret?"

Mr. Berry stood up and turned around, rubbing the back of his neck. He gave a sideways glance out the window. "That's right." His voice cracked and he quickly cleared it. "That's what I was taught and that's what I'm teaching you. Read every chance you can. Of course, there was a time when I couldn't even get a two-line part in a commercial. Both me and your mother. But look at us now. Things worked out, right?"

In a sense, Juniper thought. Her parents had received their big breaks, their dreams suddenly shifting to reality. They were so very happy, and Juniper was caught up in the thrill of it. But it was then that things slowly began to change. Juniper was still very young as her parents slowly regressed, becoming more and more reclusive the more famous they became, each year more so than the previous one. Eventually, her relationship with them was like the expanding universe; there seemed to be millions of miles between them, miles that could never be crossed, a gap that continued to grow.

And now Juniper's father kept more and more to himself, shut away in this very room reading and writing in a thick and battered journal stuffed with clippings and illustrated throughout. There might as well have been a KEEP OUT sign on the door.

Still, on this day, like every other day, she hoped to find the father she once knew. And, if she didn't, perhaps a book or two to secretly bring to her room.

Downstairs now, at the end of the long wing, she threw open the door of his study and, sure enough, there was Mr. Berry. He was pacing the room briskly. Back and forth, back and forth, his long strides never breaking. His hands were balled into fists and his head swung stiffly from side to side. As Juniper watched, his pace quickened, as did his breathing. Every now and then he smacked his fists together hard enough that the crunching sound echoed through the room. His lips were moving, but there was no sound—perhaps he was talking to himself. Juniper thought he looked like a madman.

She stood there in the doorway for minutes without being noticed. *He must be in character,* she thought. It was all she could do to keep from crying. She had said this to herself many times lately. She hoped she wasn't wrong.

"Dad?"

He didn't answer. He just walked straight to the window and peered out into the yard. His fingers scratched at the glass.

"Dad?"

Still nothing.

"Dad!" she yelled, and her father jumped. He turned around with distant, detached eyes.

"Juniper, what are you doing in here? What did I tell you? This is my space. My private space."

Wincing, Juniper took a step back, her hand reaching for the door. "I wanted to see what you were doing. I thought I could read lines with you or something. We haven't done that in a while. I wrote something new."

Although most of her plays were no longer performed, she still wrote new works daily. She wrote short stories, too, mostly about the animals she observed through her binoculars, personifying each creature into a friend she wished she had, some fantasies about the stars above or the lands at the far end of her enhanced vision, underwater worlds with large pockets of air to live and breathe in where she could talk to fish and visit mermaids.

Mr. Berry snorted. "Do you think this is a game I'm playing? I don't have time for this." He spoke faster than she ever heard him, the words tumbling out of his mouth.

"I . . . I . . ."

"Don't you have something to do, some kind of lens to look through?" Mr. Berry reared back and punched the wall. "Can't you just leave me alone?"

He dismissed her with a wave of his throbbing hand and continued with his pacing; all Juniper could do was run from the room, her heart stinging.

Mother and Father have not been right lately.

CHAPTER 2

JUNIPER COULD REMEMBER a time when her parents would never have allowed her to play in the rain. But these weren't those times, and these didn't seem to be those parents. It was as if she had new parents each year, one pair continuously traded in for the next. And so, the next day, out she went, into the rain.

Luckily, the grounds surrounding the mansion were endlessly fascinating. Almost every day, Juniper studied the creatures running in and out of the forest—raccoons, squirrels, rabbits, deer, mice, foxes, chipmunks, skunks. She observed the skies and the birds that filled it, as she, too, often wished to. In a notebook, and with the aid of a bird-watcher's guide, she marked down each of her winged discoveries: willow flycatcher, black phoebe, western kingbird, Hutton's vireo, black-billed magpie, tree swallow, oak titmouse, western bluebird, California thrasher, yellow warbler, lark sparrow, red-winged blackbird, among others. But her favorite of all was a certain raven, the blackest of all birds, as if dipped in tar, with a thick and curved midnight beak and a wide array of shredded musical communication, a bird that she could usually find on a certain branch of a certain tree in a certain corner of the yard just past where her family's property line ended, several dozen feet into the large stretch of forest.

The nearest neighbors were miles away on either side, and, for Juniper, this allowed for much exploring of the grounds. However, it also made it very difficult for her to make friends. There was simply nobody around. She was quite lonely, indeed.

Juniper knew Kitty heard the crinkling latex as she slipped on her red rain boots and coat. She came bounding in from the hallway at full speed. Man's best friend, even in the rain. *At least I have you*, she thought.

Kitty was by her side in no time, tail wagging

jubilantly. Juniper was responsible for bestowing such an unusual name upon her. The moment Mr. Berry set the Jack Russell terrier down, Juniper squealed in delight and waved her hands, saying, "Kitty!" For indeed Kitty looked like a kitten. She was similar in size and her ears curiously pointed straight up at attention—for some reason they never flapped back down as they should. Her slinky body arched and her steps were very careful in her approach to her new owner. And while her eyes were wide and bold, her snout wasn't nearly as long as it should have been. Almost every aspect of the dog stood in contradiction. It took quite some time before Juniper was convinced Kitty was actually a dog.

"Are you ready?" Juniper asked Kitty, with her hand on the doorknob. "Don't make it so easy for me this time." The moment she threw open the back door, out ran Kitty. In a matter of seconds, the dog vanished within the woods.

The game was called Here, Kitty Kitty and they played it often. Juniper would give Kitty a head start— several minutes or so—then, using her assortment of spyglasses, she tracked her down. With each new challenge, Juniper had gotten better and better, faster and faster. She would pull out her monocular to spy for a disturbance in the brush, use a magnifying glass to check for tracks in the dirt, observe the skies for fleeing birds with her binoculars. Kitty was found in no time. Usually.

This, however, was the first time they ever played in the pouring rain. For Juniper, this posed numerous problems. All the leaves and bushes and trees were already shaking and swaying, any tracks Kitty made were quickly concealed in the downpour, and the sky was empty. Still, she refused to give in and call out. She refused to whistle or clap her hands, sending Kitty running right to her. No, she'd find her if it took all day. Juniper Berry was no quitter. Besides, there wasn't much else to do.

She ventured through the woods deeper than she'd ever been, boots sinking in mud, rain pelting her umbrella, the cool air penetrating her coat. And still there were no signs of Kitty. She wasn't sure how much time passed, but she guessed that she had been searching for close to an hour. Close enough—it was actually fifty-two minutes.

On the fifty-third minute, she came upon an odd clearing. There was a pile of wood sitting directly in the center and debris strewn all about. If it had been there before, Juniper had never noticed it. At the same time, though, she heard Kitty barking in the distance. If her sense of direction was accurate—and it was—the barks were coming from the direction of her house.

Although her curiosity was strong—*who had been here and what were they doing?*—further exploration of the clearing would have to wait.

Juniper ran through the woods and back toward the house, her thoughts scattering through her head like remnants of a supernova. *She never barks like that,* Juniper fretted.

The trees whipped at her face, the mud clutched at her boots, part of her umbrella was torn, but still she pushed on. Though she didn't know why, she feared something dreadful might have happened to her parents.

Nearly halfway through the woods, her home on the near horizon still barred off by thick trunks, she saw something that immediately cleared her head of any previous thoughts. A stranger was in her yard.

Standing in the rain, flinching at each of Kitty's barks, was a boy. His hair, his most apparent feature, was a mess of brown tangles; there was so much, in

fact, that his long, thin neck barely seemed able to keep his head from tipping. Considering how skinny he was, Juniper believed that his entire body might just fall over from all the weight sitting above his narrow shoulders. Everything about him, except his hair, was small; his eyes, nose, mouth, and ears, his arms, legs, hands, and feet. It looked like he hadn't eaten in some time. He was practically swimming in his green polo shirt and jeans.

The boy did not notice Juniper standing beneath her yellow umbrella, a look of pure wonder on her face. He cautiously made his way to the nearest tree and began sliding his hands up and down the trunk. Then, when he was finished, he moved on to the next, one after the other. He looked to be deep in thought, his eyes heavily scrutinizing each tree—the rhythmic jerks caused by the relentlessly barking Kitty seemingly reflexive.

Finally, Juniper clapped her hands and the boy nearly jumped out of his unlaced sneakers. Hearing the sound, Kitty ran to Juniper's side and fell silent.

"What are you doing out here in the rain?" she asked. "You're going to catch cold."

His hand was on his heart, as if trying to keep

it from beating out of his chest. Clearly he did not expect to encounter another person on such a dreary day; either that or he was terrified of what would happen if he did. "And . . . and . . . what about y-you?" he stammered, his voice weak and whiny.

"I have an umbrella." She held it up for evidence.

"I see." The boy seemed rather sad. He shoved his hands in his pockets and let the rain drip down his face. His lips were purple and his teeth were clattering. But at least now any previous fears regarding Juniper appeared to have vanished.

Juniper's apprehension was diminishing as well. The boy obviously didn't pose any threat, not to her or anybody. She decided to follow her instinct.

"Would you like to share?" she asked, raising the umbrella.

The boy hesitated, then nodded. Juniper ran to him and held the umbrella over both their heads. Up close, she noticed he had a sweet smell about him and that his eyes captured a pattern she had never before seen, the brown and gold of his iris constantly swirling. He gave a soft smile and she liked the way one corner of his mouth ran up the side of his face while the other remained level. His fingers tapped madly against his legs, keeping time with his clicking teeth. He squirmed ceaselessly, and with every bat of Juniper's eyes he seemed to flinch. Juniper found this quite amusing and blinked as quickly as she could. He was a messy mass of neuroses. She could never have imagined a boy like this, especially when thinking up a friend for herself. Looking at him, she couldn't help but be thrilled.

His eyes kept darting away from her and she followed them to the trees at her back. "What were you looking for?"

The boy just shrugged and averted his eyes to the panting Kitty, who joined them beneath the umbrella. Hesitantly, he lowered his hand. He gave Kitty a quick and cautious pat and then immediately pulled his hand away. Kitty, eyes relaxed, seemed to enjoy it and moved closer.

"Well, you can't live around here. There's not another house in sight."

"I'm back that way." The boy pointed. "It's the next house. Technically we're next-door neighbors. Even if it does take a half hour to walk here."

"A neighbor!" Juniper couldn't contain her delight. She whipped out her monocular from her pocket, brought it to her eye, and searched in the direction he signaled. Unfortunately, there was nothing but the thickness of trees. She supposed she'd walk a little deeper into the forest during the winter when the leaves fell to get a better view. "What's your name?" she asked, collapsing the monocular and returning it to her pocket.

"Giles."

"Giles, I'm Juniper Berry. This is Kitty."

At that, Giles sneezed, covering his mouth with his hands and wiping them on his backside. Juniper promptly decided that the pleasantry of a handshake would have to be avoided for now.

"What did I tell you? Sick." She knew his hair was dripping wet, but she wanted an excuse to touch it. Reaching up, ignoring his flinch backward, she patted his head. His hair felt like thick strands of yarn or, Juniper preferred, waterlogged caterpillars. She squeezed one tangle and it leaked water into her hand. "See. You're soaked. How can your parents let you go out like this?"

"They don't care." Every word he spoke came out in a mumble, and these three were no different.

"What did you say?"

"Nothing. Don't worry about it. I'm fine."

"No, you're not. Your clothes are drenched. And why are you only wearing short sleeves?" His arms were littered with goose bumps and his skin was blotchy. She put her arm around him to warm him up.

Giles smiled at her affection, his entire face brightening like the sun on snow. Slowly, the fearful twitches subsided. "I like your hair," he finally said. "It's like it was colored with strawberries and roses." This was a close enough description of her thick and wavy hair. Usually her unruly locks bothered her, but suddenly she didn't mind so much.

"Thank you. I like your hair, too."

"You do? Nobody likes my hair."

"Well, I do."

Smiling, Giles reached out a hand to lean against a tree. Unfortunately, the slick mud gave and his feet flew right out from under him. He fell backward to the ground, splattering his clothes with muck and sludge.

"Ow!" Giles said, rubbing his bony elbow. He looked like he was trying not to cry. His lips quivered and he bit down on the lower one, revealing a chipped tooth. He turned his head and looked off in the direction of his home, closing his eyes tight. "That hurt."

Watching him there on the ground, upset, soaking wet, shivering, sloppy, sickly, Juniper couldn't help but feel terrible. "Hey," she said, "come on. Get up." She reached out her hand, and Giles grabbed it. With her hand swallowing his, she yanked him up as if he weighed no more than a pillow. He came flying, knocking right into her and nearly sending her onto the ground had he not grabbed her around the waist. She quickly stepped back and wiped herself clean, and Giles went about massaging his shoulder. "Careful," he told her, "you nearly pulled it out of its socket."

"Oh, don't be such a baby." She laughed. But, after seeing the look on Giles's face, she immediately felt bad. She couldn't believe how vulnerable he was. Everything about him, even his feelings, always seemed about to break. He looked like he wanted to disappear, and that upset Juniper.

"You're just like everybody at school," he said. "Like everyone everywhere. You looked like you'd be different. But I should've known."

"No, I'm sorry," she said. Awkward, they both looked away. Juniper could only imagine what a room full of children would do to such an easy target. She was willing to bet he would like to get as far away from everyone as possible. *That's not fair,* she thought, *there should be a place for everyone.* "Do they call you names?"

"They like to pick on me," he admitted. His face clouded over with sadness and embarrassment. "Even the girls."

"I'm sorry, Giles. Really."

"That's what the teacher makes them say. But they don't mean it. They just do it again the next day, the next time she's not looking."

"Why don't you stick up for yourself?"

"How? It's not that easy."

Juniper knew he was right. What was easy for one person was most difficult for another.

"Why don't I ever see you at school?" he asked her.

"Oh, I'm homeschooled."

Giles nodded. "I wish I was."

"No, you don't. It's incredibly lonely."

Giles looked like he was about to say something but instead looked back at the trees again, eyes searching.

"What were you doing out here?" she asked.

There was a long pause. "I was looking for a tree."

"There's lots of trees. You don't have trees down by your house?"

"I do."

"Then why would you walk so far in the pouring rain just to look at these trees?"

"I'm . . . I'm . . ." He took a deep breath. "I'm looking for a very particular tree."

"Oh." She was confused, but she enjoyed having someone her age to talk to, regardless of the odd conversation and behavior. At any rate, she assumed nothing Giles did or said could be more peculiar than what had been going on with her parents. *He enjoys nature, nothing wrong with that.* "Well, I know all the trees around here. I know every type. There's mostly pines, some oaks, firs, birches. Of course, there are different species of each. There are also junipers in here somewhere, although they're more of a shrub or small tree." Giles looked at her quizzically, and Juniper refocused her thoughts. "What kind of a tree is it? Why do you need to find it?"

"I shouldn't really say."

"But we're friends now. I'm not like those kids at school, am I?" She smiled.

Giles looked up at her. "No, I guess not."

"So, tell me, then. What were you looking for?"

He shifted his feet in the mud and swallowed hard. His eyes began to dart wildly. "I followed my . . . my parents here last night."

Juniper was taken aback. "They were out here?"

"Yeah. In the middle of the night. I'm pretty sure it wasn't the first time either. There's always something going on with them."

Juniper's eyebrows rose. "Like what?"

"I don't know, little things."

It was clear he wasn't very comfortable talking about it. His shoulders collapsed even more, his eyes shifted to the ground and didn't budge, he bit his lip, drawing the tiniest bit of blood, but Juniper needed to hear more. Suddenly she thought she might not be so alone after all.

"You can tell me," Juniper said. She thought of her ruined dinner plans. "You know, sometimes it feels like my parents want nothing to do with me. My mom and dad, they don't even sit with me for dinner anymore. We used to cook together all the time. We had Indian night, French night, Moroccan night. We'd dress up as chefs and try different accents. Dad said it was good practice for him. Now they forget I even need to eat at all. Kitty, too. She's always starving. I have to take care of the both of us."

Giles looked up at her as she continued. "Once, my

dad taught me how to do the robot." She gave a quick demonstration, arms, legs, neck, back all stiff. Then, joints popping and locking, she flowed jaggedly until slumping over as if a plug were pulled. It was quite impressive. "My mom even beat-boxed while we did it. It was so funny. But we haven't danced in so long. Every time I ask my dad he tells me his robot short-circuited or something and he can't fix it. Then things just got worse from there."

Giles glanced up at her. "And . . . and they were never like that before?"

Sadly, Juniper shook her head. "They've changed. I can't describe how exactly. It's like all the lights in the house won't turn on anymore and it's always dark, and they can't see me. Like I don't even exist. Except if they need someone to yell at." She paused, struggling with her emotions. "I used to mean something to them."

This gave Giles the courage to speak. "You're right; it's night and day." His voice grew melancholy, wistful. "They used to take me to the ocean; we used to play sports. My dad was even teaching me how to play guitar. But that was a while ago. Now even their music's different."

Something clicked in Juniper. She felt she was

getting somewhere. "Are . . . are your parents . . . are they famous?"

Giles shrugged. "My father composes operas and my mother sings. They're famous somewhere, I guess."

"Giles, it all makes sense." Juniper was trembling now. There were others like her, experiencing the same exact things. "Do you think . . . This is what happens to people like them, right?" she said. "Your parents are celebrities; they're famous. My parents—"

"I know who your parents are. I wish they were mine."

"No, Giles, you don't understand. When I was younger . . . but now . . . now everything's different. I think it's the pressure or all the attention or something."

"Maybe," Giles said, unconvinced, "maybe not. After following them, I think it might be something else. It's one thing to act mean or forgetful, it's something else to sneak into the woods in the middle of the night and . . ." He looked up at her.

Juniper locked eyes with him. "Tell me."

Giles exhaled a deep breath. "I wanted to keep a close eye on them, maybe find out what was wrong and fix it. One night, when they thought I was asleep, they left the house and walked into the woods. I followed them. I didn't want to be caught, so I kept far back. They walked for a long time, almost in a daze."

"Were they sleepwalking?"

"No. Definitely not. They hadn't slept in days. Just before they left, they were arguing like mad. Eventually, I followed them all the way here." He looked around. "I think it was here." He touched a nearby tree, inspecting it, found nothing, then went on. "Somewhere around here, anyway, and then they disappeared."

"What do you mean, 'disappeared'?"

"They were there one minute; they were in front of a tree, touching it. Then they were gone."

"It was dark out. You probably just couldn't see where they went."

"They didn't keep walking. I'm telling you. It was dark, but I was able to follow them this far. After they stopped, they just vanished."

"Are you sure?"

"I'm telling you the truth. I looked all over for them. They were gone. When I went back to the house, they weren't there. I stayed up for a long time, as long as I could, but I didn't see them until the next morning.

By then they were . . . different. You have to believe me. They were gone. Something's off. My parents . . . they . . . they . . ."

"They what?"

He clearly didn't want to say it. There was great fear in his eyes, fear that Juniper felt she understood. In fact, she knew what he was going to say, but she still needed him to say it.

Finally, he did. "They haven't been right lately."

Juniper's insides went ice cold. She looked deep into his searching eyes. "Giles, I do believe you. I really do."

The rain began to come down even harder and the thunder roared to life overhead. There was nothing to be done now. She gave Giles her umbrella for the long walk home. But not before they decided to do some more exploring together the next day, two friends in search of answers.

CHAPTER 3

J UNIPER SAT IN THE BACK ROW of the Berry home theater watching old family videos, something she found
herself doing often lately. Twelve rows from the screen,
she looked at all the empty seats before her. What were
they even there for? They were never filled, not even
close. Once, it was just the three of them, and now it
was only her. Her and Kitty.

Kitty always refused to keep still here. She preferred to run across each aisle, one after another. Up
and down, back and forth, between seats and under
them, fighting for Juniper's attention. She didn't suc-
ceed this time.

On the screen was footage from several years earlier, a trip to New York City. Juniper stood in the middle of a snow-covered Central Park with her mother. Her father's voice could be heard from behind the camera.

"Juniper, how do you like New York? Isn't it great?"

The city was quiet, the sound of traffic long faded. There was hardly anybody about and peace had settled in comfortably. Snow clung to the tree branches like white moss, weighing them down. Benches and sculptures and bridges were covered in a fine dust; the boulders were snowcapped mountains to conquer. No footprints, no disturbances, except for the snow angels they just made. The surrounding buildings vanished in a mist of white. The only guides through the buried paths were hazy lampposts, miniature lighthouses each.

On-screen, Juniper, tongue out, twirled in the softly falling snow. "We're still in New York? I don't believe it!"

Mrs. Berry laughed. She picked her daughter up and spun her around, the most beautiful of dances.

Watching this, Juniper pulled her kaleidoscope from her pocket and peered through it. The single image became hundreds.

"My two girls," Mr. Berry said. He zoomed in and focused affectionately on both their faces. He caught their eyes, then their smiles, then their whispers. "Hey, what are you guys talking about? No secrets."

Juniper nodded, both on-screen and off.

Mrs. Berry placed her down and looked at her husband. "Okay, you want us to tell you?"

"Yes, whatever you're thinking, throw it out there," he said.

"Okay," Juniper squealed. "We'll throw it out there!" And both she and her mother fell to their knees and gathered a snowball each and threw them at Mr. Berry.

"Hey! No fair!"

The camera jerked and swayed, capturing the white of New York City and the pitch of its sky and the swollen ivory moon. Laughter consumed everything, filling the speakers of the home theater.

Juniper took it all in. She looked at Kitty running up and down the aisles with her feline gait. She clapped her hands and seconds later her dog was by her side. "I don't get it," she said to Kitty. "I miss this. I miss them."

Kitty licked her hand.

"I know. They're right upstairs. But it doesn't seem like them anymore. What if . . . what if it isn't just their jobs? What if it's something more like Giles said? Do you think that's possible?"

The conversation she had had with her new friend wouldn't leave her head. It wasn't just her parents, she knew that now, but that didn't mean it was anything out of the ordinary. Giles seemed to insist that his parents were up to something strange, and Juniper had to admit roaming the woods in the middle of the night was peculiar. But that was about it. It didn't prove anything more. And yet, what did the two friends expect to discover together? Surely, Giles's parents didn't just disappear like he said.

Kitty turned on her back, exposing her belly to be rubbed. Juniper obliged, then answered her own question. "No, I suppose not. I suppose this is what happens when people have more important things to worry about than . . ." She trailed off.

Just then the theater door swung open and her mother stood in the entrance, hands on hips. In the odd mixture of light and shadow, along with the flickering of the screen, she looked like a different woman. Juniper didn't know if this was a good thing or not.

"Juniper! Get out here right now! Your tutor is waiting for you!"

Mrs. Maybelline—Juniper nearly forgot. "I was just watching this." She pointed to the screen. "Remember this?"

Mrs. Berry glanced at the screen for no more than a second. "Of course I do. New York."

"But—"

"Get out there now! This woman follows me around and why? I'll tell you why: because you're not out there. Don't you know I have far better things to do than run around looking for you? If I don't nail this part, there are thousands of women waiting to pull me from my perch. It all can fall apart so easily. And what if that happens, Juniper? What then? Go back to years ago? Back to that little house, living those little lives?"

"Why not?"

This set something off in her. Mrs. Berry charged at Juniper and yanked her out of her seat. Kitty barked wildly. "Why not? Why not? Are you serious?" She was shaking Juniper now, digging her nails into her daughter's arms, a different sort of dance.

Juniper's head thrashed from side to side, tears were gathering in her eyes, and still her mother continued.

"You don't understand!" There was something missing in her eyes. They weren't the same as the beautiful pair on-screen.

"Mom," Juniper cried. "Mom, what's wrong? Tell me. Please. No secrets."

Mrs. Berry sneered. "No secrets? Well then, here it is, Juniper. The truth." She pulled Juniper's face close to hers, each one's nose only centimeters from the other's. Mrs. Berry's teeth were bared, her nostrils flared, and her eyes were dark. Then, in a distorted guttural voice, she said it. "I've finally got what I want. And I'm not going to let it go."

And with that, she pushed Juniper out of the room and toward Mrs. Maybelline in the living room.

Coughing, nearly gagging, Mrs. Berry went back upstairs, a strange jerk in her walk. The lovely gait of years ago was gone. Now she was smaller somehow, slightly hunched and crooked.

Juniper wiped her tears and sat beside her tutor. It was all she could do.

"She talked to me today," Mrs. Maybelline said, her eyes wide and giddy. "Your mother. She said, 'You. Wait here. I'll get her.' Oh, it was wonderful just to be in her presence. I couldn't even talk. I must have made such a fool of myself."

"She seemed normal to you?" Juniper asked. Even though it was someone to talk to, she didn't grow attached to her tutors anymore. They never lasted very long. Her parents always found some reason to get rid of them, even with the confidentiality agreements all employees were forced to sign.

"Normal? Oh, no no no. There's nothing normal about your mother. Or your father."

Juniper inched up in her seat. "There isn't?"

"Not at all. Why, they're . . . they're . . . stars!" Mrs. Maybelline couldn't even blink. She stared off in complete awe.

Juniper sighed. "What are we doing today?"

"You can be like them, too, one day. You're very talented, Juniper. I see it. Your writing is top-notch. Top-notch. Plus, with their connections . . ."

"I don't want to be famous. I don't want them to be famous either."

Mrs. Maybelline found this hysterical. She guffawed with every ounce of her rather large being, her cheeks reddening, her veins pulsing. "Kids"—she laughed—"you have to love them." She continued laughing, her bulbous body bouncing jollily. Juniper couldn't look away. It was quite a sight. Mrs. Maybelline was right; she saw nothing but stars.

But then, almost instantaneously, the laughter stopped. It just cut off mid-ululation. Something had caught her eye. "Oh my God," she whispered, pointing down the hall. "Your father. Oh, wow."

Juniper turned and saw her father staring out a window just like he did in his study the day before. Enraptured, he didn't move. Juniper knew what was out that window, she used her monocular out it many times. It was a straight shot, an unobstructed view. Right into the woods.

Mr. Berry continued staring, his hand reaching out for something that wasn't there.

Mrs. Maybelline didn't find any of this odd. "He's so dreamy," she wheezed. "Juniper, you are the luckiest girl in the world. To have parents like that, I swear."

"Mrs. Maybelline?"

No answer.

"Mrs. Maybelline!"

"Huh? What? Yes?"

"Are there . . . are there things out there . . ." She nodded ahead. "Are there things that can change almost everything there is about a person? Something that can make people become like my parents?"

Mrs. Maybelline was still caught in her stare, but she responded in a wistful voice. "I sure hope so. Whatever it is . . . I want it."

The lesson began and the lesson ended, and Mr. Berry never left that window.

CHAPTER 4

With her mother and father about to leave for rehearsals and all lessons completed to Mrs. Maybelline's empty satisfaction, Juniper was on the roof. She was sprawled out on her stomach letting time tumble by as she anxiously waited for Giles to arrive and their expedition to begin. The pulsing sun, attracted to the dark paint of the roof, warmed her back as she spent the slowly expiring minutes spying with her binoculars on the crowds outside the gate. It was a favorite activity of hers.

People stood enraptured at the gate, peering in, searching for a sign of the Berrys. There were fans of

all ages—the word "fan" derives from fanatic, Juniper's father often informed her lately—a wide spectrum of life and ethnicity, some of whom slept in their cars or pitched tents outside the estate. They were but a small sample of a world Juniper hardly knew, and she couldn't have been more intrigued by their every movement and gesture. Focusing on their mouths, as she had done so often, she attempted to read their lips, following the conversations she so desperately wished she was a part of. She used their body language to guide her, whether they were laughing and waving their arms or if they appeared awkward or angry, friendly or flirtatious—sometimes conversations don't need words, she realized.

Through her binoculars she read the homemade signs and collages. She followed the zooms of the arsenal of camcorders; she watched the camera phones extend through the gates for the best picture possible, while other people turned the lens on themselves making sure to get the house in the background. These pictures, it appeared, were immediately sent somewhere, thumbs busy on the keypads. It occurred to Juniper that, as much fascination these people had for her family, they had an equal amount for themselves and especially their phones. Some hardly ever glanced up. She couldn't understand why they wouldn't, with so many people around to talk to.

Mingled throughout the masses were the ever-present and persistent paparazzi. In a seemingly endless cycle, they lurked, steadfastly orchestrating the fanfare and spectacle. And so Juniper, for her own safety, was told by her parents to keep far away from life outside these gates, lest she be exploited, tormented, or worse.

After turning around to quickly scan the yard for Giles—unfortunately, there was still no sign of him—she returned to the crowd and watched as two kids, who couldn't have been much younger than herself, raced each other from one end of the street to the other. *That could be me*, she thought, and then quickly realized that she had never been in a race before. *How is that possible?*

Seeing all this day after day, everything these people had, all they could do and experience, the entire world waiting to be explored, Juniper wondered why they wasted their time hoping for just a brief glimpse of a family doing something so dull and ordinary as advising a gardener on certain shrubbery or walking from the front door to the car. Why were these moments to capture?

Searching the crowd for an answer, she spotted a woman—she, too, with binoculars. Only, it seemed this person was looking right at Juniper.

Finally! Contact! Juniper offered a small wave of her hand and a gentle, welcoming smile.

"On the roof!" the woman screamed. "On the roof! The kid! Their little girl! Juniper!" She let out a searing squeal and soon everyone was pointing and shouting and screaming. Flashes went off, the paparazzi scrambled, the gates shook. People shoved their way to the front.

Although she was at a safe distance, Juniper's heart thrashed.

Suddenly security was at the gates, pushing the crowd back. But it wasn't for Juniper's sake. Mr. and Mrs. Berry's car was coming through.

As the black Bentley wheeled past the gates, the roar of the crowd grew. Their hands slapped at the tinted windows. "Who's in there?" they shouted. "Which one is it?" Then, as if in response, Mrs. Berry's hand emerged from a crack in the rear window and waved. "I love you! I love you!" the crowd shrieked, loud enough for Juniper to hear all the way on the roof. One fan jumped on the hood of the car and had to be forcefully removed. Some were actually crying. "You're the best!" "Stop, please!" More pounding of palms against the windows and doors. Hands extended markers to sign their pictures and T-shirts, cameras clicked away madly.

Finally, the car drove off, the gates closing automatically behind the chaos.

"I don't understand any of this." Juniper had seen enough. It was time to find Giles.

By the time she crept back through the attic window, walked down two flights of stairs and out the back door, Giles was sitting on a tree stump watching the ax man chop some more firewood on the far side of the yard. Giles looked to be in awe at the power of each swing, the crack of blade splitting wood with ease.

"I was going to call you, but . . . look how fast he goes," he said as Juniper approached, never shifting his eyes. "It's like the ax is a part of him." He grabbed at his own biceps and frowned.

"That's Dmitri," she told him, hands still grasping her binoculars although they were attached to a strap hanging about her neck. "He does a lot of work around here."

Hearing his name, Dmitri stopped, looked over, and waved. He was a big man with a large dark beard speckled with gray, brown, and orange, and massive arms and shoulders. After wiping his brow, he spat on the ground, dug his heels into the dirt, and went back to work.

"Do you think we can talk to him? I'd like to be able to do that, become as big as him." Giles turned to Juniper but kept glancing back at Dmitri.

Juniper, however, had more engaging thoughts on her mind. She grabbed Giles by the arm, noticing that her hand could almost close entirely around it. "I've been thinking about what you said yesterday," she told him. "Maybe you were right to follow your parents, maybe they're up to something in the woods."

"You think so?"

Juniper thought of her parents' strange behavior from the previous day and all the days leading up to it. "It's possible."

"But where did they disappear to?" Giles looked around, his hand displaying the sprawl of the woods. "It could be anywhere. We could search for days."

"True," Juniper said, "but I have a place to start. Right before I saw you yesterday I was exploring the woods with Kitty. We were playing a game. She hides and I try to find her."

"Like hide-and-seek," Giles said.

Juniper looked blankly at him. Hide-and-seek sounded familiar, maybe, but she certainly never played it. No, she played Here, Kitty Kitty. "Well, I couldn't find her for the longest time, and just when I came across a clearing, I heard her barking. Someone had been out there, but I never had a chance to inspect it because of Kitty. I went running and that led me to you."

"You never went back to check it out?" Giles asked.

Juniper shook her head. "But we can now. Together."

Without another word, for they were understandably quite eager, they made their way into the woods.

It took some time for Juniper to remember where she had gone, but, searching for evidence of her steps with her magnifying glass, she eventually found the clearing.

Nothing whatsoever grew within this curious circumference. It was as if a perfect circle had been burned into the middle of the woods. She had never seen anything like it before. Giles appeared similarly perplexed.

In the center of the clearing, drawing their gazes, were the remainders of a campfire. Slowly, Juniper and Giles approached the soggy woodpile. *Who was all the way out here?* Juniper wondered. *Stalkers?* Her parents had had more than a few problems with overzealous fans recently.

Kicking at the charred tree branches, she noticed some debris sprinkled about. It appeared to be burned paper. She crouched down and picked up one of the scraps, part of a journal—there was a portion of a date at the top, April something or other, but because of the fire and rain the rest was indecipherable. She picked up another, as did Giles. Nothing could be made out. Then Giles came across yet another page, this one mostly intact. They looked it over. Some Roman numerals and random symbols, none of which meant anything to them. Juniper shifted more of the wood. There! A page with writing. She snatched it up and began to read.

Walls are walls are walls
And what we see is what we see
See?
Up and over is the only way

To an ornery new world
Not round and round and round (we go)
There is no either/or
Tranquilized eyes, I saw—
Oh, please, I must have a sickness
The sun'll come out tomorrow, tomorrow, won't it?
From such heights, one can only fall
HURRY UP PLEASE IT'S TIME
It always is even when it shouldn't
It always is even when it couldn't
Mememememememememememememe
These aren't my thoughts
I don't know my self

The words terrified her. They were gibberish, mad ramblings. But this wasn't the part that set her stomach fearfully tumbling.

"This is my father's handwriting," she said. There was no doubt this was true—the way the letters leaned and swirled, the faint punctuation—and yet there was not a trace of her father within them. What did it all mean? Why was he out here? She thought he might be trying to hide, but from what? What was happening to him?

"Juniper, the back." Pointing at the paper, Giles looked bewildered.

Juniper flipped the torn page. On the back of the journal entry, scrawled across the top, she noticed the same numerals and symbols from the previous paper. And below that was a sketch of a very particular and striking bird.

"I've seen this bird before," Juniper said. "It's a raven."

"I'm sure there are lots of them in these woods."

"Not that I've noticed. I've seen only one around here." Her eyes met Giles's. "And I know exactly where to find it."

Juniper led them back through the woods and to a tree near where she and Giles had met the day before.

It was an ugly tree. If any were to be chopped down, it should have been this monstrosity. Its branches were bare and sharp, reaching out as if to pierce the sky, although the sky certainly did nothing to instigate such an assault. The tree, not incredibly thick, not incredibly thin, was riddled with knots and odd twists, roots that ripped the ground, killing the grass and welcoming the weeds. Nothing else grew from the base all the way to the top. There was nary an insect crawling across the trunk or a squirrel nesting in the branches.

However, there was the raven. Juniper looked up at it, wanting to say hello, and the raven seemed to nod. Its feet were wrapped around its usual branch, wings tucked comfortably to its sides, eyes fixed on the two children.

"Is this what my parents were searching for?" Giles asked. "This tree? Do your parents know about it, too? They must."

"I don't know. It couldn't be a coincidence, could it? But I don't get it. What would they want with a dying tree?"

Circling the trunk, they both began inspecting. They yanked on branches, kicked at roots, pressed each knot, clawed at bark. Finally, Juniper pulled out her magnifying glass for closer inspection. Giles watched her. "Why do you have all those things?"

"What things?" Juniper asked as she continued her investigation, her lips pursed and tight in concentration.

"That magnifying glass, those binoculars around your neck. Yesterday you pulled out a telescope-type thing."

"A monocular," she answered without glancing up.

"Yeah, a monocular. Why do you use those things?"

"I . . ." Juniper had to halt her examination for a moment as she thought this over. What was it she loved so much about these possessions? She was never asked before. While nonchalantly flipping the magnifying glass in her hand, she turned to look directly at Giles. "When I look through them I see . . ." She had to search for the right word, for words are very, very important. "I see the truth."

"The truth," Giles repeated.

"They can be very truthful. They bring everything closer." She glanced at her surroundings. "That cloud doesn't really look like that and neither does that ant and neither do the stars or the moon or you or me or anything else we see, for that matter. These let me see the smaller parts that make up everything else, the things that are hidden right before our eyes. I don't know. What I like most of all is that they bring the world closer to me." She shrugged, feeling like she might have rambled on too long and sounded ridiculous. "They're my spyglasses."

"You like to spy on things?"

"I like to explore. There's so much out there to discover." Speaking of which, she went back to inspecting the tree.

"For you, maybe." Giles looked toward the sky with such a penetrating glare it was as if he wished to see right through it. "I think I found out all I'd like to know about this world."

"Too bad it's the only one we've got," Juniper joked.

Giles didn't laugh. "Maybe not. There has to be something else out there, something better."

Juniper didn't know how to respond to such a sad statement. *It's odd,* she thought, *he wants out of the world and I want in. Is there something in between?*

Her fingers traced a groove in the side of the tree, and she immediately focused her magnifying glass over it. "Look at this."

"What is it?" Giles asked.

A voice answered from behind them: "That's from Betsy."

The two friends turned to find Dmitri hovering over them, ax slung over his shoulder. There was a sudden rustling and they all watched as the raven took to the skies, screeching a disturbed tune. Dmitri eyed it suspiciously. Soon it was out of sight, who knows where and who knows if it was still watching.

"Betsy?" Giles asked, staring at the blade.

Dmitri extended his ax. "Betsy."

Giles hesitated for a moment, then grabbed it for a look. The blade immediately fell to the ground. Beet red from both embarrassment and effort, he struggled to remove it from the soil.

Juniper questioned Dmitri. "You gave it a name?"

"Well, people give all types of nonliving things names, don't they? Cars, guns, rocking chairs."

"Guitars," Giles offered as he finally pulled the blade free, nearly sending himself flying backward.

"Careful now," Dmitri urged before continuing. "That's right, guitars, too. Coincidentally, guitars are also called axes, and are usually given female names. So I figured I'll give my ax a name."

"You chopped this tree?" Juniper asked.

"Just one swipe. It's an ugly tree. I wanted it for firewood for your family, but your father stopped me. He came running from the house. He was furious, eyes practically red. Told me to keep to that side of the yard, never to touch this tree. I've never seen him like that. Since then I've learned not to interfere, as much as I would like to. Some lessons have to be learned on one's own."

"What do you mean?"

Dmitri opened his mouth, then closed it quite

suddenly. His eyes went to the part of the sky in which the raven had fled as he pondered something for a few moments—for some reason people always seem to believe the answers are right there above them. No doubt, Dmitri was debating something. Finally, he shook his head and, with his hand, retraced the mark his ax made in the tree. "This one's ready to come down. This is the sweet spot right here. Just a few solid downward strikes and a ratty old tree like this will tip. I won't be sorry to see it go, that's for sure." He pulled back his hand and wiped it clean on his pants. Juniper did not fail to notice his arm was covered with goose bumps.

Dmitri retrieved his ax from Giles and threw it down into a stump, where it lodged. "This is where she sleeps; don't wake her up now." He smiled without showing any teeth. "I'll be on my break. Try not to get into any trouble, you two."

He walked away and Juniper and Giles could only stare at each other. Dmitri's words seemed to linger in the air, even the ones he didn't say.

Juniper ran her finger across the mark once more. Her father stopped him from chopping it down. Why?

The search for explanations continued a while

longer—Juniper setting up a tight perimeter to explore—but nothing was discovered, no revelations of any kind. What was the connection between her parents and Giles's? What was the meaning of the scrawled ramblings and symbols, the clearing, the tree? They had to be missing something, but what?

After nearly an hour more, that missing something still wasn't found. Exhausted and out of ideas, Juniper decided they should break for the day. However, at this point, neither she nor Giles wished to part company.

"I don't have to be home yet," Giles said. "Doesn't seem like I have much of a curfew anymore."

"Well, there's still plenty of day left," Juniper pointed out. "What would you like to do?"

"What do you usually do?"

"I'm usually alone," she admitted.

"What about all those people outside your gates? You never made friends with any of them? They must be dying to meet you."

"Ha! My parents would never go for that. I'm not allowed anywhere near them. My dad says they're crazy, but I think he's more concerned with lawsuits and bad press."

"No, he's probably right," Giles said. "But I'm sure they'd like you. You're smart and pretty." He turned away. "They'd just mock me."

"That's not true. Why would you think that?"

"It's okay. I'm used to it. Look at me, all scrawny and weak. There's a reason why those people wait outside for a glimpse of your parents. They all want to be just like them. Nobody wants to be like me, and you know what, I want nothing to do with them. I wish I could just leave, just get out of here and never come back. I never need to see anyone ever again. I mean it."

This hurt Juniper. She wanted to ask if he meant this about her, too, but kept quiet.

"I can live by myself," Giles went on. "I know I can. Only problem is, in this world, people are everywhere."

Except here, Juniper thought.

"We can have our own little world, Giles. Right here."

He laughed at this. "Sounds good. Our own planet. Until I have to go to school again."

And so, for the rest of the day, living in their own world, each had a friend in the other.

Even without much experience in friendships, the lonely girl and the castaway boy filled the time as two friends should. In fact, it so delighted Juniper to have a friend she nearly forgot the tree entirely. The reminders were never very far away—two of the biggest were lurking within her house—but for the moment they remained in the background.

Juniper led them on several insightful expeditions to the outlying areas of the yard, although not anywhere near the clearing. Through a variety of lenses they spied even more birds and animals making their way in the world, documenting it all in her notebook. "Can I see space with these?" Giles asked, scoping the sky with her binoculars.

"Not even close. I have a telescope in my room, though."

Giles was excited. "Can I see it?"

Eyes to the ground, Juniper answered, "My parents wouldn't allow it."

"Oh." Giles pulled at the loops in his jeans and rocked on his heels. "Can you see far with it?"

"The telescope? Really far. I've seen meteor showers, the phases of Venus, lunar craters, and, because I have a solar filter, sunspots. I've even seen the shadows of Jupiter's moons on its surface."

"Wow, really? Just think what else is out there."

"You don't have to go far. I've seen just as much in an anthill."

Giles's eyes searched the ground for one. Quietly, he began to sing. "'Next time you're found with your chin on the ground, there's a lot to be learned, so look around.'" Catching himself, he suddenly stopped, embarrassed.

"What was that?" Juniper asked.

Giles blushed and fidgeted. "Nothing. A song my mom used to sing to me. I forgot all about it until now."

"You have a nice voice."

Giles smiled, then stopped, his eyes suddenly sad. "We used to sing together, the three of us. My father gave me his record player—he says records make music sound more emotional—and we would sit around and sing old songs. I miss that." Giles froze and looked gravely at Juniper. "Are our parents going to be okay?" His voice shook.

Just hearing such a question made Juniper's entire body go cold. She didn't know how to respond. She could only grab his hand and give it a soft squeeze.

They shook these fears free by keeping busy. They tracked Kitty through the woods, Juniper informing

Giles on how to proceed in such a quest. While wearing goggles, they scanned the shaded depths of the heated pool for sunken treasure and did flips off the diving board. With a microscope, they examined a ladybug. They played hide-and-seek, which Juniper found to be no different from Here, Kitty Kitty except that Giles said she couldn't use her spyglasses. It was as if they had been friends for years.

At dusk, just before Giles left to go home, Juniper suggested one more activity. "I want to have a race. One end of the yard and back."

Giles looked intimidated. "Does the loser have to do something embarrassing?"

"What? No. It's just for fun."

Having agreed, at the starting point Giles asked, "Are you fast?" and Juniper responded, "I have no idea."

Raising his arm, Giles announced, "On your mark, get set, go!" for Juniper didn't know such protocol existed. They kicked their legs to the limit, these two, a fury of speed. Giles was quite fast indeed, and Juniper was surprised to discover that she was, too. In mere seconds they made their turns at the halfway mark and headed back for the finish line. Juniper grinned the entire way. When it was over, they hugged and said good-bye.

As for a winner, it was decided that the race was too close to call.

But if one were to possess a keen eye, as Juniper did, the outcome was evident: She won.

CHAPTER 5

JUNIPER HAD AN IDEA, and that idea morphed into a plan, and that plan was put into execution, and that execution was taking place presently. It was well after bedtime. Blanket pulled to her chin, head caught in the plushness of her pillow, she was asleep. Or at least she appeared to be, for this was part of her plan. She could just barely see out of the tiniest of slits she had made of her eyelids, and what she waited to see were shadows in the hall, just outside her door, coming for her.

She didn't have to wait very long.

With the rain pounding against the window, growing heavier by the minute, she watched the stretch of darkness reach her bedroom door. They were here.

Juniper had formed the plan earlier that evening, shortly after Giles left. It was Kitty who sparked it. She was trembling before Juniper, whimpering uncontrollably, her sad eyes glassy. In rapid bursts, she scratched at Juniper's legs, then took off down the hall.

Curious, Juniper followed.

A minute later, she found herself outside her father's study. The door was open and the moaning from inside was audible. "Oooohhh. Oooohhh." It sounded painful and caused Kitty to retreat, most likely beneath some blankets or sheets, where so many have fooled themselves into believing they are safe—it was okay, she had done her job.

Stepping into the room, Juniper saw her father lying on the floor. He was on his back with his arms and legs stretched wide like a fallen star, staring at the ceiling. The moaning suddenly ceased and, quietly, eerily, he began to sing damaged, twisted notes that crawled from down his throat in a scratching grind and grew to a near shriek:

I don't know what's right.
There's nothing in my head.

Nothing in sight.
There's nothing in my head.
Nothing but white.

I am me, but I'm not me
I'm not me, but I am me
I am me, but I'm not me
I'm not me, but I am me.

Then, clutching his stomach, he went back to moaning in the voice that didn't seem to be his own. "Oooohhh. Oooohhh."

"Dad?"

Sharply, Mr. Berry turned his head but appeared to look right through her. His eyes frightened Juniper and, heart pounding, she took a quick step back, ready to run.

"Yes, Juniper?" he said, and the words were distorted, her name battered into a guttural absurdity. To Juniper, it almost sounded like two different voices overlapping each other, his own and something else, something otherworldly. He swallowed and coughed, nearly gagging.

"Are . . . are you okay?"

"No. No, I'm not," he whispered, his voice slowly returning to him.

"What's the matter?"

"I'm lost. The character . . . he won't come to me. Or he will and he won't go. I don't know anymore. The pieces don't fit together."

Juniper couldn't understand; her father had starred in dozens of movies, and he was so greatly admired, by none more than her. She glanced over at his shelves of awards—two Oscars, four Golden Globes, dozens of critics prizes. He never struggled like this. Never.

"Can I help?"

"No. I'm afraid you can't."

"Why not?" she asked.

He turned back to the ceiling, raised his arms, and pulled at his auburn hair. "Forget I even said anything. Go tell your mother I have to talk to her. Hurry. This can't wait much longer."

Then, with his arms in the air, fingers tugging away at large clumps of hair, his sleeves fell to his elbows and she saw marks, red marks that sent her stomach plunging. "Dad? What's that on your arms?"

Mr. Berry quickly pulled his sleeves down and sat straight up, glaring at her with damaged, volcanic eyes.

"I said go!" he screamed.

Hurrying off, Juniper couldn't help but think about Giles's story of his parents. Something was wrong, and she needed to find out what. She clenched her fists. A plan would be needed.

Juniper waited until her mother closed the study door, then began to search for the best spot to hear their voices. Once she found it, she placed the rim of a dinner glass against the door. Ear to the bottom, she closed her eyes as if this would make things even clearer. Soon her parents' words found their way through the wall and into the glass.

"How long has it been?" her mother asked, her words only slightly muffled. "I feel like I'm losing track of time."

"Just hold out until tonight."

"We're doing the right thing, aren't we?" Mrs. Berry coughed viciously. She sounded horribly sick— not that Mr. Berry was concerned.

"Do you even have to ask? It's the only way."

"You know I hate going there."

"Are you trying to tell me it's not worth it? Would you like to give up everything we have? Go back to . . . to . . ." Mr. Berry couldn't complete his thought.

"To our old lives?"

"I can barely remember that life. Can you?"

"There isn't much to remember, is there?"

"No. No, I guess not. All the more reason to—"

There was a crash. Moans, commotion. Juniper's heart raced as she tried to decipher the sounds.

"Inside . . ." It was her mother's voice. "It hurts so much."

"Get up. Fight it. It's getting dark. It'll be time to leave soon enough."

Juniper had heard all she needed. She fled to her room.

In the hall, hours after this incident, with the plan finally taking effect, the shadows stirred. Juniper pulled her blankets tight and forced her eyes closed. There was a quiet creak as the door was pushed slowly open. Then, a short moment later, her father's head peered into the room. He gave a quick scan and whispered, "She's sleeping. We have to go now."

Mrs. Berry pulled her husband away from the door. "We need this. It means everything. I think I'd die without—"

"Keep your voice down. She'll hear. We can't have her involved. Not ever. Now, come on."

And with that, the shadows chased her parents away.

Juniper, completely dressed, shot up in her bed as if poked by a very sharp and perhaps scorching stick, reached over to her nightstand, and grabbed her binoculars. Taking a deep breath, she moved to the window. Outside, the yard was eclipsed by darkness. Then she brought the lenses to her eyes.

The newest addition to her spyglass collection was the night-vision enhancement to her binoculars. It was something she'd wanted for a long time and had received it on her most recent birthday in a blue box handed to her by the chauffeur with a tag reading *Love, Mom and Dad.* She still received gifts for such occasions as her birthday and Christmas and so on, but her parents, like on most days, usually weren't present.

And now she was going to find out why.

She scanned the yard, waiting for a glimpse of her parents in the pouring rain. The world appeared to her in shades of green—there was lime and olive, chartreuse and viridian, jungle green, electric green, spring green, and midnight green. But, amazingly, everything was clear. With infinite detail she saw the trees and grass and the night critters and the gazebo and the plump moon and the drops of rain splashing the pool water. She saw the world as if it were lit by a neon green sun.

But still, there was no sign of her parents. Was she actually mistaken? Was there no connection between her parents' behavior and the tree she and Giles had inspected?

Her bedroom door creaked back open.

With a gasp, she turned. Stretching across the carpet toward her was a shadow, a feline-shaped shadow. Juniper let loose a sigh of relief. It was only Kitty. There was comfort in seeing her dog, knowing she wasn't alone, and she was pretty sure Kitty felt the same.

Kitty jumped onto the bed. "I know you can sense it, too," Juniper whispered, giving her a quick stroke. "I've seen how you've been avoiding them. It's okay, though. I'm going to figure all this out." With that assurance, Kitty curled into a ball on the pillow and Juniper returned to the window. Just in time, too. There her parents were, running to the trees with their jackets pulled over their heads, the yellow beams of flashlights splitting the darkness. "See," she said, "I knew it."

With her sneakers already on, Juniper ran out of

the room, down the stairs, and to the back door, Kitty close to her heels. Quietly, she pushed the door open and, just as Giles had his own, followed her parents into the woods.

The rain flattened her hair and her clothes were instantly drenched, but that didn't slow her. Stealthily, she tracked her parents; she darted around tree after tree, keeping her knees bent, body low to the ground, but there was no need: They never looked back. Through her night-vision-enhanced binoculars, she could see how intent they were on reaching their destination.

With Kitty in tow, Juniper found the ditch she dug several summers ago as part of her personal excavation site—she was in search of fossils or treasure or both—and dropped into it. Elbows propped up on the level ground, she spied on her parents trekking through the mud and brush. All that could be heard was the plopping of raindrops upon the black tarp lining the hole. The trees shook eerily in the moonlight, branches extended and wavering like tentacles. All animals, aside from Kitty, had sought cover long before. Juniper turned to look at her loyal companion beside her. "This is it," she said.

For her parents, it wasn't even a search. They knew where they were going; they ran straight for it, straight for the tree, the very one Juniper expected them to reach. Sure enough, sitting on its favorite branch, even in the downpour, watching Mr. and Mrs. Berry gather round the trunk, was the raven. It flapped its wings and screeched into the midnight darkness.

Through the binoculars, Juniper watched her parents. They somehow looked relieved, even happy, happier than she had seen them in what felt like years. Under a pale moon, they bore the smiles she had long wished to see.

Mr. Berry pushed against the trunk and, a moment later, his wife walked behind the tree in a crouching position and was gone. She didn't appear on the other side or farther back in the woods or anywhere else, for that matter. She simply wasn't there anymore. Juniper leaned forward. "Giles was right," she whispered.

Mr. Berry then followed her into the void, as did the raven. There was some type of threshold just behind the tree, there had to be, something just out of sight beyond which they could disappear. Juniper, refusing to lower her binoculars even to rub her eyes free of rain, waited.

As the ditch filled with water, a series of questions rumbled through her head at a rapid pace. If there was a door out there, where did it lead and how did her parents ever discover it? How long had they been going to the tree? What kept them coming back? Why didn't they tell her about it?

She had her own answers to all these questions, but they weren't proven, so she quickly dismissed them. Guesses and gossip and suspicions were never good enough. No, as she had learned, she had to know the real answers, the truth, and to get them she would have to discover them herself.

The rain pelted her skin. She was shivering, her teeth clattered away, goose bumps ran across her body. *This is what Giles experienced,* she realized. *Except I'm not going anywhere. I'm waiting for them right here.*

Twenty-eight minutes later, Juniper's parents, much to her excitement and distress, finally came into sight. There one moment, then gone, now back again. It was as if they had risen from the dead.

As they made their way from the tree, their marker into the void, Juniper saw something trailing after them, writhing in the night air. *Is that . . . it couldn't be.* Trembling, she focused her binoculars on the floating objects. Yet what she saw didn't make sense; any and all logic must have been washed away by the rain. There, in her father's left hand, and one more in her mother's right, were balloons. Green and violet balloons, on strings, like one would see at a carnival. Together, Mr. and Mrs. Berry walked through the woods like lost children.

Juniper finally pulled the binoculars away from her weary eyes. Her heart was beating ferociously. Her hands trembled. *What is going on? What is this? What is happening?*

It was time to find out.

With her parents back in the house, Juniper climbed out of the ditch. Kitty, perhaps sensing fear or danger or something more, whined. "No," Juniper whispered, "I have to do this, Kitty. I have to know."

As quietly as she could, dripping wet, Juniper opened the back door and went inside. It was an hour when only the house was supposed to talk with its creaks and cracks and ticks and tocks. Yet in reaching the hall, her sneakers squelching softly, she heard whispers. She couldn't make out any of the words but managed to follow the wisps of sound around several corners.

Her parents were in the dining room.

Down the hall she skulked, moving at a careful pace toward them, until she could hear their conversation clearly.

"Are you ready?" her father asked with a shaking voice.

"I hate this part," her mother replied.

Juniper crouched all the way down and extended her neck much like a turtle to peer into the room. Her parents were seated at the table, one on either end, holding the balloons to the granite surface with both hands as if about to eat them. Their eyes seemed hungry, but their tense bodies appeared to be working against them.

"It's for the better. It's for our future. We need this."

Slowly, her mother nodded.

"At the same time, then. On three." Her father began to count, "One . . . two . . . three." And up the balloons went to their mouths, their hands frantically undoing the knot. Ravenously, they began to suck the air from inside.

It was the noise that brought Juniper to her feet. They slurped the air like soup, except the pitch grew and grew, turning the air into a mighty wind down their throats.

Without thinking, Juniper ran into the room. "What are you doing?!"

And that was the moment she knew real fear.

Her mother turned to her, her face nearly melting, the skin bubbling from beneath, and screamed at her in a voice of utmost horror. "Get ooouuuutttt!" The words sounded strangled, deep, like a straining and damaged foghorn. Her mother's eyes were no longer her own; they bulged grotesquely, yet the irises shrank away. Her mouth drooped and sagged as the air of the balloon found its home inside her body, her skin turbulent like boiling water. Bestial moans crept from across the table. There, her father's head was leaning back, eyes to the ceiling as if satisfied, yet his legs shook violently and his body twitched. Not once did he turn to his daughter.

The veins in her neck pulsating viciously, Mrs. Berry screamed again, "Get ooouuuutttt!" And Juniper fled the room.

CHAPTER 6

After a night of little sleep and much fear, Juniper warily descended the stairs. Already, something was clearly out of place. She smelled the wafting scent of eggs and heard the sizzle of a skillet upon the stove. She made her way through the house and entered the kitchen on an orange-skied morning. Her mother and father were at the table eating breakfast, with nary a word passing between them. But there was no doubt Juniper entered a room humming with plenty of good cheer.

"Wonderful to see you're up," her mother said. "We've saved you some." She pushed a plate of scrumptious scrambled eggs and sausage toward a dumbstruck Juniper. "Eat up, eat up, eat up," she cooed.

Confused and cautious, Juniper took a seat, closely eyeing her parents. They seemed pleasant enough, not a glint of shame or guilt in their actions from the previous night. Mrs. Berry was smiling and Mr. Berry was whistling; he even gave a wary Kitty some eggs, something he never did, saying it was good for her coat. Did they even remember what had happened only hours earlier? Now, in direct opposition to their previous night's state, they were filled with energy, their skin shining, their bodies humming. The only thing that betrayed all of this was their eyes. The glow Juniper remembered seeing in them as a young child had nearly faded completely. Was this just yet another version of her parents?

"This is delicious," Mr. Berry told his wife. "This is just what I needed today. So much work to get done. I finally know how to tackle this character. I can hear his voice as clear as my own. It's as if he's pushing and shoving to get out. This is going to be my greatest work yet. I just know it." He clapped his hands, then pumped his fist into the air a bit awkwardly.

Juniper turned to her mother, who began to speak quite merrily. "Well, the work we do, you have to start your day like this." She scooped some eggs onto a piece of toast and took a large bite. "Rehearsals start at noon. I have absolutely no fear anymore. I'm sure they'll be heaping accolades upon me in no time. I can already hear the whispers. Listen." And everyone went silent, even Kitty.

"Award talk. I'm hearing award talk," Mr. Berry said, hand cupping his ear and grinning.

"I know, for the both of us."

"It's always nice to suddenly wake up with a new perspective on things. The heaviness of life is gone. I feel light. It's like I'm a new man."

"Everyone should be as lucky as us."

"I can't sit around anymore," Mr. Berry said, rising from the table. "Let's get this day started."

"Yes, let's."

And Mrs. Berry joined her husband in exiting the room, leaving Juniper sitting at the table, speechless.

She didn't know how to respond to any of this. She wanted to ask questions about everything; she wanted to say, *Aren't you going to explain what it was that happened last night?* But she knew she would be wasting her breath.

Either they would have denied it ever occurred or they had already chosen to believe it never actually did. And maybe it didn't happen at all, not to the two people in front of her. With her face flushed and her eyes still puffy and red from a restless night, she knew; it was going to be up to her to set things right.

She had to get back outside and explore that tree.

But first she would have to push through another day of lessons with Mrs. Maybelline.

It turned out to be a test day—something Juniper completely forgot in all the perplexities taking over her life. Not that it really mattered; Juniper was an excellent student, and there hadn't been a test yet that she had failed to ace. In fact, sitting alone at the kitchen table, she completed the two-hour test in just over forty minutes—that included checking her answers twice for careless mistakes, of which there were none.

She never told Mrs. Maybelline how quickly she breezed through these exams, and this allowed her to be free from her tutor's gaze for the full two hours. Meanwhile, Mrs. Maybelline just so happened to hand out tests quite frequently because it gave her the chance to roam the house and try to get a firsthand glimpse of the private lives of her favorite celebrities.

Juniper had a feeling she wouldn't last very long at this job. But this was the least of her concerns. Right now she was busy looking out into the yard and what lay beyond it.

Binoculars around her neck, she walked across the lawn until she was in the best position to get a glimpse of the tree but without wandering too far from the kitchen window. Hoping to find something, anything, she and Giles might have missed, she spent a full hour of her test time searching for a neglected clue. But, unfortunately, however long she looked, nothing came to her. All the books she read, all the adventuring and exploring she conducted, it all proved useless. She and Giles had searched nearly every inch of the tree and now it stood there silently, unwavering in the breeze, revealing nothing. There was just that same raven perched on that same branch.

Juniper focused on the bird's jet black frame. "You never go very far, do you?" she whispered. "What is it about that tree keeps you coming back?"

Sometimes talking things out, even if only to one-self, can lead to astounding conclusions, as it did here for Juniper. Regarding the tree, she noticed, the raven was the only variable. She remembered it flying off when Dmitri approached, she recalled it seemingly greeting her parents the night before, and she was sure every creature in those woods avoided that tree, all but the raven. Suddenly she got the feeling that it had something to do with finding the entrance. It had to. What else was there? And, in a whisper, she said, "Show me."

Beyond the yard, on that certain branch, the raven's head bobbed and turned, looking in several directions. At one point it seemed to glare directly at Juniper. *Did it see me?* she wondered. *How?*

Shrieking, it fluttered its wings, arched its body, and pecked at the trunk. After a brief moment, it took flight, circled, and vanished behind the tree.

"It's the raven," Juniper said in disbelief. "That's the key." And with that, a chill crawled up her spine.

Later that afternoon, with Mrs. Maybelline having just left minutes earlier, there was a knock at the back door, a very soft rattling of the screen. *School would have let out about an hour ago,* Juniper thought, checking the clock. *It must be Giles,* and she came charging down the stairs to greet him and inform him of her discovery. However, someone else reached the door before her.

"Who are you? What is this?" Without waiting

for a response, Mrs. Berry grabbed Giles by the arm and yanked him back into the yard, where she began to scream for all her employees to hear. "Who let this boy on my property? Does anybody care about my safety anymore? What do I pay you for!"

Dmitri, halting his work as the other workers scattered, approached with his arms extended, palms up in a calming manner. "No, Mrs. Berry, you have it all wrong. He's—"

"I have it wrong? I have it wrong? How dare you! I'll put you back on the street in no time!" She shook Giles by the arm, her nails puncturing the skin. "Do you have any idea how many people would love to gain notoriety through me and my family? Snapping photos, spreading lies! We are targets!"

Knees weakening in pain, Giles cried out and pleaded for release. "Mrs. Berry, please . . ." but Juniper's mother paid him no mind.

"Mom, wait!" Juniper called, running from the house. Her binoculars, hanging around her neck as usual, beat against her chest with each stride. She saw the tears welling up in her friend's eyes. "You're hurting him!"

"Get back, Juniper. It's not safe." The good cheer

of the early morning was long gone, a bright mirage against the darkening day.

"Mom, that's Giles. He's my friend."

"A friend? You of all people should know better." Her head darted viciously from side to side. "He's jealous of us."

"No, Giles isn't like that. I swear."

Mrs. Berry glared at him, licking her lips and snapping her pristine teeth. "Perhaps not yet. Give him time." She patted Giles down for a camera and, finding none, shoved him toward Juniper. "And you"—she pointed to Dmitri—"get back to work. I don't pay you to stand around, do I?"

"No, ma'am." Sheepishly, Dmitri retrieved his ax from its stump and continued his chopping without a second glance back.

Mrs. Berry turned to Juniper. "You keep an eye on this one," she said, referring to Giles. "He is in great despair. I see it." She then hurried into the house holding her head, as if it were expanding.

"I'm sorry," Juniper said to a teary-eyed Giles, who was busy massaging his arm.

"Don't worry about it, June."

A nickname. Juniper was overwhelmed. She

approached him and rubbed her thumb beneath his eye—something she remembered her father once doing for her a long time ago. "Don't cry," she said.

Then, looking closer at her friend's flustered face, she gasped. His tears were falling from a grotesque black eye. "Oh my, did my mother do that to you?"

Giles shook his head and sniffed. "School."

No more explanation was given, but no more explanation was needed; Juniper had an idea or two.

She gestured toward her house. "My mother never used to be like that," she told him. "Everyone used to love her. She treated everyone so nice."

"It's the tree," Giles said with a croak. "Right? Same as my parents. That's what's causing this."

"We're going to find out." She then proceeded to tell her new friend everything, from her parents' journey into the wet, dark night to their balloons to their surprising good cheer the following morning to her theory about the raven.

"Do you really think a bird can help us?" he asked about her plan.

"I think we don't have anything else to go on right now."

The setting sun left the sky bruised, and the light

breeze became a cutting wind. Juniper and Giles returned to the decrepit tree and were greeted by the roving eyes of the raven. It flapped its wings wildly and let out a piercing screech, the loudest yet. Juniper gazed at it for some time, wondering if what she was about to do was crazy or not. Finally, she said, "We want to enter. Please, show us how."

Immediately, the raven flew down and perched at the top of the trunk. It screeched some more, once at Juniper, once at Giles.

"Is it trying to tell us something?" Giles asked incredulously. "Are you actually talking with it?"

Intently, Juniper stared at the raven. In her stories animals talked all the time, and the real world was just as fantastic a place as anything she could create; it never ceased surprising her, so why should it now? "How do we find the entrance?" she asked again.

The raven squawked an odd song and pecked its beak at the tree several times.

"There?" Juniper asked. There was no groove in the spot, no dent or knot or scratch. It looked no different from any other part of the tree. She pulled out her magnifying glass and studied the area. And indeed there was a mark. It was very slight, almost unnoticeable, just a mild discoloration, as if the tree had bled a long time ago and scarred. No wonder she had passed over it when they first looked. "There?" Juniper asked again, pointing.

The raven screeched, appearing to nod once more.

"It can understand us?" Giles asked.

"We'll find out," Juniper answered.

Making sure Dmitri was well out of sight, Juniper exhaled a deep breath, swallowed whatever fears festered, placed her finger against the mark, and pushed.

CHAPTER 7

THERE WAS A NOISE, an unusual sound, as if the tree were speaking gnarled words. The ground trembled slightly, the raven flapped its wings, and yet nothing appeared to change. Perplexed, Juniper continued to stare, waiting for something, anything, to be revealed. And, sure enough, something was.

From behind the tree, Giles let out a startled gasp. His eyes were focused downward; his jaw hung slack.

Juniper followed his mystified gaze. In the bottom of the tree was a gaping hole, opening into the ground like a black mouth.

"Stairs," Giles muttered.

Juniper collapsed into a crouch and leaned her head closer to the hole, peering within. "It's so dark. They look like they spiral and twist, but I can only see a few of them."

"Do . . . do we go down?"

As if in response, the raven took flight, whizzing past their faces and down into the darkness, an echoing cry left for them to follow.

Juniper turned to Giles. "We go down."

She placed her foot on the first cracked step, and a nauseating chill crawled up her ankle. Her entire body went cold.

Ducking her head and taking a deep breath, she took a step beneath the tree, then another, gripping the earthen walls for balance and guidance. Large insects crawled up and over her feet and across her hands. Spiderwebs clung to the walls like clouds. "Don't let me do this alone, Giles."

"I'm right behind you," he said, and to reassure her, he reached out and put a hand on her shoulder. Juniper, warmed at the touch, reached up and grabbed it.

The two friends moved slowly, unable to see the steps in front of them, the light of the outside extinguished in mere moments as if someone had squeezed the sun out. They didn't know how long they were descending, but it felt like hours. For Juniper, time seemed to have halted, or stretched into something immeasurable, incalculable. Maybe down here there was no time.

"What if these keep going forever?" Giles asked. "What if we can't ever get out?"

Juniper feared that as well and then remembered, "Our parents got out. So will we." But did she really believe that? How could she be sure the ones who emerged were the same ones from years ago?

After what seemed like an eternity, there was a shuffling of light creeping up the stairs. The walls seemed to move within its soft glow, and, after a few more steps, Juniper had reached the bottom.

There was only one direction in which she and Giles could go, and that was down a large hallway that stretched into further darkness. The only light came from four torches, two on either side of the hall. It was eerily quiet, the only sounds being the whispers of the flames.

The raven flew from out of the distant darkness, hovered before them, squawked, then turned and flew back from where it came.

"Are you ready?" Juniper asked.

Giles was shaking, but he nodded his head and they

began to venture down the hall, following the path of the bird.

There were six doors in all, three on each side of the hall, all evenly spaced. They were massive wood doors with ornate carvings in each. Juniper and Giles stopped at one, inspecting it closely. A marking of an owl filled a large portion of a panel. The predator's wings were extended and its claws were open. Just out of the owl's grasp was an image of two keys crossed and, below that, spread between hieroglyphic-like symbols, were two sets of Roman numerals:

III XXIII XL V VIII XII
XIII XIV LXI IX XX LII

Seeing this, something buzzed within Juniper's head. She had come across these images and numerals before. Reaching within her pocket, she seized her father's charred journal entry. Flipping over the absurd ramblings, she saw the same exact markings scrawled on the back.

Juniper decided to check the door directly across the hall.

The carved panel on this door confounded her

even more. It revealed a many-pillared building with a sun shining through it chasing eight little pigs from within. Below that was what appeared to be a lion, but with a snake as a tail and a goat's head protruding from its back. It had a man pinned beneath its body. He appeared to be dead.

"Chimera," Juniper whispered. "It's Greek mythology, I think."

"What's this?" Giles asked, pointing to another door on which a sheep was tethered to six balloons, floating through the sky. Something dripped from its body, falling like rain to form a lake in which a hooded man stood rowing a small boat. There was another series of Roman numerals and symbols written in the lake, the identical markings from the previous door and, again, matching her father's writing.

"I don't know. Let's see what's inside. Open it up."

Giles pushed against the door, his feet sliding backward in his tremendous effort, but it only budged slightly. "I can't," he said. "It's heavy."

Juniper stepped in front of him and put all her weight forward. After much strain, the door began to give. Giles looked away, embarrassed. The bottom of the door rubbed against the ground, adding much resistance, and Juniper had to pause to gather more strength. Staring at the opening, she wondered how long it had been since the door had last been opened.

From inside, something began to move closer, something that scraped across the floor at a torturously slow pace. Juniper and Giles were frozen in fear. As the noise grew louder, the grating sound stood their hair on end. Then, pushed through the opening, came a bowl, empty except for a small amount of brown water. A long wooden stick shoved it a few inches farther and Juniper noticed that something was dangling from the middle of the pole. It was tied with string and was no more than two inches in length but seemed to be moving, swaying. It appeared to be in the shape of a person. Could that be right? She reached out, but the stick was pulled away, leaving the bowl in the opening.

Juniper and Giles exchanged curious, frightful glances. Then they heard the noises coming from within.

There was a gurgling sound and a wet slap, as if someone were tossing a bucket of slime against a wall. It repeated in a timely fashion. But there was an even worse sound mixed in among this. It sounded like the voice of a very old man croaking his final breaths: "Salhack . . . Salhack . . . Jup nen skek. Salhack . . ."

Then, worst of all, was the hiss. "Pleeeeeaaaasssee . . ."

Juniper went to push the door open even farther, and at that moment a blinding light blazed from inside. "What is it?" Giles asked, shielding his eyes. "What's in there?"

Before Juniper could answer, before she could even peer through the glare, the raven screeched past them. It flew into the room shrieking and rasping, causing a great and puzzling commotion. There were more indecipherable words, a scream, agony. The raven flew back out and pecked at Juniper and Giles until they returned to the middle of the hall. The door closed on its own.

Seemingly irritated, the raven flew down the hall, then back again. It repeated this several times until Juniper and Giles followed obediently. It was clear they wouldn't be able to conduct any further investigations, for the raven was intent on leading them somewhere.

Following their winged escort, Juniper and Giles approached a cavern of sorts. The torches were fading behind them, along with the six doors, and a new light burned softly in the coming room.

A voice emanated from within. The coldest, most peculiar and frightening voice they had ever heard.

"You have found me."

CHAPTER 8

A͟PART FROM A LONG TABLE at which sat the shrouded figure with the wicked voice, the room was a barren chamber lit by two torches. The ceiling dripped what Juniper assumed to be rainwater, and shadows upon the walls shifted and danced in the flickering primal glow. Every now and then she could swear they formed images—dark, disturbing images that lasted just long enough for her to question if she even saw them at all. She couldn't help but feel that the shadows were of an altered, twisted world and wanted nothing but to consume her.

Beyond the room there was another hall, this one

kept in complete darkness.

As Juniper and Giles entered the room, the man stood. He was extremely tall, taller than any man Juniper had ever seen. In fact, almost everything about him had length. Each body part was extended: long legs, long arms, long neck, long fingers. He was enveloped in a ratty hooded cloak, his elongated face concealed in shadow. His bony pale fingers wrapped around a wood staff, and Juniper noticed his nails were long as well, and dark, as if painted midnight blue. As the shroud pulled tight against his body with each movement and gesture, it was clear how very feminine it was. There seemed to be no fat whatsoever and little muscle— a fragile, lank, and stretched frame. Barefoot—his feet were nearly skeletal—he leaned against the staff, hunched over and shifting all his weight to one hip. He was a gangly creature, and would have seemed close to the point of breaking if it were not for how he slithered about, his limbs like anacondas in their movement.

The man, if he could be called such a thing, stepped closer, slinking his way toward the children, his face still hidden but for a smile that glowed like moonlight. It was all teeth, long, yellowed teeth that stretched his

purplish lips wide across his face—a twisted triangle of sneering terror. "I'm so glad you came," he nearly squealed.

Juniper didn't know what to say for she wasn't glad to be in that room with him; far from it. She considered running, fleeing for safety, but convinced herself to remain if she wanted to help her parents. She had to be brave even as a fearful voice repeated over and over in her head, *He has too many teeth. He has too many teeth. He has too many teeth.*

The raven flew over to the man's shoulder and settled.

"My name is Skeksyl. This is my raven, Neptune. And you are . . . ?" He pointed at Juniper.

She didn't want to answer, but her name somehow slipped free from her lips. "Juniper."

"Ah. Of course." He looked at Neptune. "He's told me about you for years now. He assured me you'd one day pay me a visit." The raven uttered some croaks and garbled notes, and Skeksyl turned back to Juniper. "He's a very smart bird. I take it you already communicated with him, but did you know he can actually speak? To some people. The special ones. They can hear his voice trickling between their ears like a conscience. What a privilege it is. He tells me he'd like the two of you to get to know each other. He says you are a very, very interesting girl."

To this, Juniper could only stare. Something about his voice simultaneously soothed her mind and agitated her soul. He was a paradox.

"Don't be so shy. It just so happens I'm a dear friend of your parents. Both of yours. But you already know this, don't you, Giles?" Incredibly, his smile grew even larger, as if new teeth suddenly popped into existence.

Giles swallowed bitterly and nodded. His knees were nearly knocking together and his face paled.

"Giles and Juniper. Juniper and Giles. Are you here to have your dreams come true as well?"

Quizzically, the two friends looked at each other. "We . . . we're here for our parents," Juniper said, finally.

Skeksyl smiled even wider, if that was possible. "Oh, Juniper, I can give you two much more than that. I have the ability to hand you everything you could ever want but believed to be unattainable. There will be no doubt. There will be no obstacles anymore, no pitfalls or setbacks. Your parents are great talents all, but they couldn't fulfill their destinies alone. No, they needed a hand. Mine." He laughed a sinister squeal of a laugh, a high-pitched lunacy that shot through the room, chilling it. "You see, I pull dreams into reality."

Juniper and Giles exchanged dubious glances.

"Ah, but you'll want proof," Skeksyl said, detecting their hesitation. "You'll want a little taste. Of course. Come."

With Neptune taking flight, Skeksyl walked past them and back down the hall, stopping before the first door, this one with a carving of an overflowing chalice with people swimming in its liquid. Or were they drowning? "Step through this door and by the time you reemerge, there will be no doubts in your minds. What you see in this room I can make a reality. I will show you your dreams in a handful of dust."

Effortlessly, their grinning guide threw open the door and waved them through.

The room was black: the walls, the ceiling, the floor. Blackness layered upon blackness with blackness between. The door closed swiftly behind them, and they could not see each other or even their own hands before their eyes, let alone a way out. They were confined to the dark, and all was silent.

Juniper had to speak to make sure she wasn't alone. "Giles?"

His voice found its way through the dark. "Did

we make a mistake?" He sounded very close, and a moment later she felt a hand grasp her arm and slide down until they locked fingers. The touch was delicate, heartwarming. At that moment she didn't need her vision; she knew it was him. Her hand tightened its grip.

It wasn't a surprise that she could feel Giles trembling, sending a wave of quivers from his body to hers. For both of them, there was much fear, much in question, their only comfort being that they had each other.

"It'll be okay. Everything will be okay."

"What if he doesn't let us out? What if this is a trap?"

But Juniper had no chance to respond. In the following seconds came the sudden sensation of falling. She was sure of it; she was in free fall. Her hair flowed behind her, and the air rushed past her face, whipping the clothes on her body and the skin of her cheeks. Any sense of direction was immediately and utterly destroyed in this riddle of a room. She didn't know if she was upside down or right side up or where the door was or if she was even anywhere near that room anymore. She was tumbling through dark air, head over heels, the bottom pulled out and never replaced.

And yet it was a serene feeling. Strangely, they were lulled into total ease, and neither spoke, taking it all in: the utter weightlessness, the complete freedom. Juniper felt her problems fading away, her concerns crumbling. They could have been infants once again, safe and gently rocking. It was so tempting to just give in to it.

Minutes gave birth to even more minutes, and still they fell and still nothing came into view. If they had room for ominous thoughts in their tranquil minds just now, they would wonder if it were possible to fall forever. Would they sleep while falling, grow while falling, live while falling? And if they ever did land, what would happen to them? *Splat?*

But such fears never entered their minds, and they eventually came to a stop. They didn't land on anything; there was no crash, not even a jerk, just an ease into rest, as if falling into zero gravity.

And sure enough, with hands still clasped, Juniper and Giles were floating, and all around them were millions and millions of stars.

The light allowed them to see each other's shocked faces, the awe stretched across both. Although it should have been freezing, the twinkles of the stars warmed their very bodies, head to toe, inside and out; although they should not have been able to breathe, each exhalation was exhilarating. They were in the depths of space.

Shockingly, without the slightest hint of a sound, a massive space station streamed by, floating as if it weighed no more than an air bubble. It passed them by, the size of a small city. They could see every detail, every bolt, every scratch, the streaks in the paint, the astronauts within—a true marvel of humanity.

Then, while turning in the dead of space to follow the station's path, Juniper and Giles found something even more spectacular. Looming oh so large behind them in all its magnificent glory was the Earth.

It was a powerful moment, one that would never be forgotten. In the thick of space, the swirling orb was so peaceful. All the problems of Juniper's life, all the news transmitted daily from every TV and computer, the flicker of a billion screens large and small, none of it existed up here. Only beauty and stillness. Such a sight made her heart swell, a sensation to end all sensations. It had the power to make one believe in anything, like a dream floating in space.

Juniper was awestruck. It was the most beautiful

thing she had ever seen, and instantly she knew she had to share this experience with others. People had to know. Witnessing such a sight . . . it changes lives. She tightened her grip on Giles's hand. Was it true? Had they really left Earth?

At unimaginable speeds they began to fly through space, gliding past the moon and out into the farther reaches of the solar system like tiny meteors each. They soared with the starlight and yet nothing was a blur. This was life outside of lenses.

They reached Mars in mere minutes, floating past the red rock-strewn surface, spotting NASA spacecraft digging through the soil, mapping the planet, searching for evidence of water. They circled Jupiter, peering into its roving red spot and seeing the lightning crash incessantly within. That spot alone, Juniper noticed, was so large it could fit three Earths inside, while the planet itself was larger than one thousand. Such size was beyond humbling. Jupiter was coated in horizontal layers of clouds, each one circling the gaseous globe in separate directions and speeds like the turn of screws, as if the planet were somehow unlocking.

They journeyed through the asteroid belt circling Saturn, which they discovered was composed of icelike particles, some as big as a car, some the size of pebbles, caught in orbit, remnants, perhaps, of a former moon. Uranus and Neptune, too, they noticed not long after, were wrapped in rings, albeit much smaller in scale. In silence they passed Pluto, and Juniper thought, indeed, it was not a planet.

They traveled to the edge of the solar system and beyond, witnessing worlds upon worlds, extraordinary colors and shapes, stardust and meteors, moons and comets, asteroids, red, brown, and white dwarfs, gas giants, solar flares, pulsars, quasars, galactic halos, nebulas, celestial objects that rattled the imagination.

Holding hands, they raced past stars and through galaxies, the happiest they had ever been. "This is a miracle," Giles said. And to Juniper it did seem like that. A miracle. But was that the truth?

And it was that question that moved her hands to the binoculars around her neck, setting the night-vision enhancement. For once, however, it was difficult to bring the lenses to her eyes—what would she see? She didn't want to ruin a good thing. But she had to know the truth; she had been tricked and duped enough in her life. Her parents were no longer her parents, and she didn't want to be fooled anymore.

Slowly, she raised the binoculars to her eyes.

Through the lenses, the expanding universe vanished. She saw the very same four walls in which they first entered. Beside her, Giles wasn't floating but standing still. They'd never even left the ground. It was a copy, an imitation. As genuine as it seemed, it wasn't the real thing. *When this theme park ride is over, we're going to walk out the same door we walked in.* There was no miracle.

Sadly, she thought, *Is there even such a thing?*

Suddenly, as if she were a bolt of light from an exploding star, she was hurled through the universe. The speed was incredible, eliminating all sound, and she had no idea if Giles was still beside her. She dropped the binoculars and was again in space, passing the planets in reverse, heading directly for Earth like an asteroid. The blue-and-green swirls of her home began to take shape. As she burned through the atmosphere, the surface became larger and larger. She flew closer and closer. Or was it a fall? She passed through the clouds like lightning, and the ground rushed up at her. Juniper shielded her face with both hands. There was going to be a horrendous crash. She could see the mountains and rivers, the cities and buildings, then the houses, then the streets, then . . .

She was standing on a carpet. Hundreds of people surrounded her. Sound slowly returned and she could hear the crowd's joyous screams. Both her hands were held by someone on either side. She looked up into the warm eyes of her parents.

Cameras went off and her father picked her up and her mother kissed her cheek, telling her to wave to their fans. With the largest of smiles, Juniper did so; she waved. She waved so much her arm tired. Above her, in equal-size lettering, the marquee displayed her name beside her parents': WRITTEN BY JUNIPER BERRY. Everything was aglow, and Juniper believed her eyes shined brightest of all. Overwhelmed, she trembled with lost emotions.

Her parents escorted her up the steps and to the movie house. Just inside the entrance, dozens of microphones were thrust in Juniper's face. Her audience wanted a statement.

Juniper took a step forward. She looked back to her parents, who nodded and smiled, their eyes filled with nothing but love. The microphones extended farther. The crowd quieted. Juniper, nearly in tears, craned her neck forward and talked through a Cheshire-cat smile.

"This is what I always wanted."

And with that, the faces vanished, the light dimmed, and Juniper and Giles were back where they started. All around them were blank walls, an empty shell of a room.

The door creaked open.

In the faint torchlight, Skeksyl awaited. "So, are we ready to negotiate?"

CHAPTER 9

≡

WHEN JUNIPER AND GILES returned to the cavern-
ous room, two chairs were added to the table and, like
the table, they were made from hand-hewn tree limbs.
On the table surface were four shrunken balloons
neatly aligned in a short row. Neptune, perched upon
his master's chair, gave careful watch over the deflated
latex.

Skeksyl walked eagerly to his chair, his staff thump-
ing the ground with each slinky stride, and took his
seat on the far side of the table. With a wave of a gaunt
hand, he suggested Juniper and Giles join him, which,
after only slight hesitation, they did.

When all were seated as comfortably as the chairs would allow, Skeksyl began in that grating fey voice of his. "What did you think of the experience? Thrilling, no?"

"Unbelievable!" Giles shouted.

Like a pendulum, Skeksyl's bony finger swayed, negating the jubilant comment. "No, no, no. Very believable. As believable as anything else you've ever seen. It sits waiting for you, Giles; it sits on the very edge of your reality. Now all you have to do is give it a push. Send it on over. Make it so."

Neptune, now on Skeksyl's shoulder, squawked and fluttered his wings without taking flight, a mad mascot. The gesture made it seem as if he were applauding Giles.

"How?" Giles asked. He inched to the edge of his seat.

"First, you choose who you want to be. You have seen but a glimpse of what I can offer you. One aspect of millions. So easily the two of you can possess such gifts for yourselves." He turned to Giles, fingernails digging into the table hard enough to leave marks. The wood came up in curls as he dragged his hand back. "Giles, you were satisfied with what you saw, were you not?"

Giles nodded.

"Well, what would you like? Who do you want to be?"

"I want to be an astronaut." Giles made a quick glance toward Juniper. "I want to leave Earth behind and see space. Like in that room."

Instantly, Juniper saw all the pain Giles suffered, all the taunts at school, the bullying, the isolation, the desertion of his parents. He really did plan on leaving everything behind.

"Of course. And you will. Boy, I can guarantee it. You will discover worlds others have never dreamed of. There are places that will see you as their king, places with populations you can crush beneath your feet. There are planets so mesmerizing you will completely forget about this insignificant one. No longer will you be neglected and ignored. You, Giles, are destined for far greater things."

Skeksyl giggled wildly, and the shadows flickered as if joining him.

"Oh, I can give it to you. All that and more. But an astronaut? Now? At your age? That particular gift would be of no use to you. You are still far too young to be allowed such privileges in that world of yours. A shame, really. The imagination of the young is nothing to be dismissed—if only I could get my hands on those in charge. Alas, for that aspiration you must return to me when you come of age. Another handful of years or so. By then you will be ready for that tremendous journey. You will reach the stars, I promise you. Of course, I'm sure we'll have had many exchanges by then, preparing you step-by-step. But, tell me, what can I do for you now? What do you want changed immediately? This very day."

"It can be anything?"

"Anything." Skeksyl's smile grew as he stretched the word into a multitude of syllables.

Giles looked down into his lap where his small hands were neatly folded. He raised them and looked at his palms, his thin wrists, his sticklike arms. Without glancing back up, he said, "I want to be strong. I don't want to be pushed around. Everyone laughs at me. If I'm going to stick around here for a while, I don't want to be made fun of anymore. I want to be able to stand up to them."

"Giles," Juniper said, "you don't need that, you—" but Neptune screeched a deafening screech, drowning out her words.

"Ah, strength," Skeksyl said, his fingers dancing across the wood table. "Juniper, you do not know what horrors and torments this boy experiences. Just look at that black eye. You don't want to be a target anymore, Giles, and I don't blame you. Strength is an admirable trait to possess. Wars are won with strength. Mountains climbed. Beasts felled. There are no weak heroes, are there?" With a finger he gestured to Giles, who turned his head toward the blackness beneath Skeksyl's hood, from where his voice emanated. "People admire strength. Girls admire strength."

"He's still young. He'll grow," Juniper interrupted. But it struck her how small her voice sounded.

"Grow? When?" Skeksyl asked her. "How soon? How can you be so sure his body won't fail him? Alas, Giles, it is always so simple for someone to say from afar. Especially a pretty girl. You live with this plague, not her. Look at you. Shriveled, weak. Ridiculed daily. I can change all that. And I can do it now."

"Please," Giles uttered. He looked at Skeksyl, at the shadows on the wall—anywhere but at Juniper.

"Certainly, my boy." Skeksyl clapped his hands, and Juniper was surprised not to hear an echo. Down here, every sound but his vexing voice died a quick death. He lifted two of the balloons by his dark and sharp fingernails, a red one and a blue one, and placed them directly in front of Giles. "Which one would you like?"

Timidly, Giles pointed to the blue balloon.

"Of course. The color blue is a favorite of yours, is it not?"

Giles nodded.

"I had a feeling."

From within his cloak, Skeksyl procured a quill. It was a black feathered quill, as if plucked from the wing of his pet raven. He spun it between two fingers, rolling it back and forth as he licked his lips. On the blue balloon, with the perfect penmanship of a master calligrapher, he wrote the word "strength." Placing the quill down, he brought the latex to his lips and blew the balloon whole, tying it into a knot and attaching a string, all in a flash, all with incredible ease. When finished, he picked the quill back up and offered it to Giles. His hand trembled; both their hands did. "All you have to do is sign your name on my balloon. Sign your name on the red balloon and blow it up with the fresh, youthful breath from your lungs," he squealed in his warped singsong voice.

"That's it? That's all I have to do?"

"That is all."

Giles barely hesitated. He snatched the quill from Skeksyl's quaking hand and awkwardly signed his name.

"Now fill it," Skeksyl repeated. "Blow it up big."

Giles picked up the red balloon and finally turned to Juniper.

"You don't have to," she mouthed.

He looked at her pleadingly for a moment, then brought the balloon to his lips. Juniper turned away and closed her eyes.

In a few large breaths, the balloon was full.

Instantly Skeksyl snatched it from him. He knotted it, tied the string, and wrapped it several times around his emaciated hand, squeezing it tight as if it were about to blow away in a vicious storm. Exhilarated, he beamed a broad smile from within his hood. His chest heaved, he nearly panted. "Now listen closely. When you get home you open that balloon. Don't let any of the air escape unless it is down your throat. You must inhale it all or it won't work. Do you understand?"

Giles nodded.

"Good. Very good. The world will be yours soon

enough. Whenever there is something that troubles you, whenever you find something in your way, don't panic. There are ways to overcome. There is nothing simpler."

Slowly, he turned his attention to Juniper. "And now for you, Juniper. What would you like, hmm? I have made actors and dancers, politicians and athletes, scientists and philosophers. What do you want, what does your soul ache for?"

"I'm happy the way I am."

Skeksyl's laugh sounded like a banshee's shriek. "Noble, indeed, but I have yet to meet a person happy with what they were given. Even the most adored and idolized have their desires. As you grow you will see how quickly the world can leave a person behind. It can beat you down. It can be brutal. There is no easy path in life. None at all. Except . . ."

The walls flashed their images, and Juniper found herself staring into them. A single image blazed through her head, the same jubilant scene she had wit-nessed in that empty room just moments ago. She was with her parents and they were happy. The three of them laughed and smiled like the family they had once been. A lump grew in her throat.

Averting her gaze, Juniper clenched her hands together. "It's . . . it's nothing like Giles's wish."

"It doesn't have to be. You and Giles are different. Each person's dream is their own glorious universe. Dreams do come true, but only for those who know how to seize them. That's why it is so rare. Most can't do it without help, without certain assistance and manipulation. I can show you the way."

She knew she should keep her mouth closed, but the temptation had already crept in. Her parents might not ever return to being the mother and father she remembered. In the end, even her own life might not become what she wanted it to be. Just eleven years into it and already it wasn't what she hoped for. No friends, no family. She wanted someone to share her stories with; she wanted to feel how she believed a child should feel. None of that had happened, and she couldn't be sure this would ever change.

Yet, this promise, this was something. It was too late to change the past, but her future was wide open. There was still a chance to bring her family back together the way it was when they put on her plays, and perhaps this was it. And so she spoke.

"I want to be a writer."

Skeksyl jumped up. "Read all over the world! Your words recited and lived by! Your name remembered for lifetimes! My dear, the worlds Giles visits you will see just as clearly. They will live in your head. This locked-up world will come alive for you. And, unlike Giles, we can start you out young, this very day. With such a head start you can become the youngest writer to ever pen a film, your name up in lights. Surely your parents couldn't ignore that, could they?"

The shadows danced more wildly now. Skeksyl turned, taking them in. When he faced Juniper again, he was smiling with understanding. "The family business. You can create roles for both your mother and father. You can be the one responsible for their next awards. How proud they will be of you. A true family, inseparable. They will return to you because you will finally be what they always wanted you to be. Soon people all over the world will love you for what you will give them. And with power like that, you can live whatever life you desire. You want to be a writer? I can help you become the greatest to ever live."

Juniper now knew the truth. Skeksyl had given her parents exactly what they wanted; they achieved all their dreams. There was no going back for them;

Juniper knew this. But now there was a way she might be able to come along as well.

But was that why she was here? She could hardly remember anymore.

Skeksyl folded his hands atop one another as if to keep them still. "Do we have a deal? Is this what you want? Tell me and I'll make it so."

There was no doubt the temptation was great. It was all she ever wanted. She could reunite with her parents and, as long as she could breathe, the wishes would be granted. Suddenly she saw it all before her, all her dreams, everything she could ever want, carried in a balloon.

But if her parents made their deals, why didn't they seem happy? Or maybe they actually were happy, maybe their happiness was different from hers, like what she witnessed in that room floating past the stars, whether they were real or fake: It's all relative; it's perspective. Happiness is happiness. If she didn't have her binoculars, there would have been no signs that they weren't really in space. She could have made herself believe it, couldn't she? What was real? What was truth? What was happiness? She wasn't sure anymore. Could it be different for everybody?

She glanced at the balloon Giles clutched so tightly. What was in those balloons anyway? What was floating around in that magical air? She had seen what such a gift did going down her parents' throats, and it frightened her, even if they returned to the tree for more. It was doing something to them, something horrible. That was real, that was the truth.

"No," she said in an unwavering voice.

"No? What do you mean, 'no'? I'm offering you a future of dreams. Do you know how many people would do anything to be in the position you are in right now?" Skeksyl's hands shook once more.

"I said, 'No.'" She sounded strong, but inside she was coming apart. Was she giving up on her parents? The thought terrified her.

Skeksyl sat back, calming. "I see. You're not convinced. Not yet. How about another venture into that room, hmm? It can show you anything, everything."

"It wouldn't matter." Juniper shook her head and glanced down at her binoculars. *When I look through them I see the truth,* she had told Giles, and she believed that. Going back in, she knew she would only see an empty room.

Skeksyl followed her gaze. In a flash, his staff shot

out, hooked her binoculars, and lifted them from around her neck. The strap slid down the staff and the binoculars fell into his opened hands. "Oh, Juniper, you think this is the answer?" he asked, holding them up. "You think spying through this will tell you everything you need to know about life, about people? The only truth is the one we create. It's the rest that is a dream. You can break everything down, analyze it all you want, inspect, investigate; it doesn't matter. You won't *belong*. Wake up, Juniper! The facts are fiction, the truth is fantasy. You think your binoculars bring the world to you? You foolish girl. They keep you out. Like a spectator, you watch from a distance, and as long as you watch you'll never participate. Give up trying to make sense of it all. It isn't what lies deep down that matters but, rather, what you show to the world. Don't you understand, the world wants to be fooled. Flash the colors! Make a fuss! Puff your chest! Give them the show, Juniper. It's all they want, and they'll eat it up ravenously. There's nothing beneath the surface, nothing hidden or out of sight; everything you need to know is all right before you. What is there to understand but how much you're missing? That is all you can learn from such devices. Nothing more.

This . . ." He held the binoculars high. "This is your weakness." He gave the binoculars back to Juniper, and already they looked foolish in her little hands.

"You'll return. Of that I am sure." He smiled at Juniper, then at Giles. "Both of you will. Come back anytime, as you are always welcome here. Where else can that be said of the two of you?" He waved them toward the hall. "Go now, I'll be waiting."

And with that he walked out of the room, down the other hallway. The thick darkness enveloped him instantly, the bright red balloon he carried the last thing to fade.

CHAPTER 10

IF WE ARE DOOMED to repeat history," Mrs. Maybelline said, "then we might as well make it fun."

"Fun?" Juniper asked, her voice lost in a haze. She could not follow her day's lesson adequately, as her mind constantly drifted to Giles. She had not seen him since they emerged from beneath the tree four days ago, and now she missed him greatly. For hours she waited outside, monocular outstretched, searching the distance for her friend. But he still hadn't appeared.

"Yes, fun!" Mrs. Maybelline shouted. Her girth swallowed the edge of the desk, and a pudgy hand opened Juniper's laptop computer. With a strike of a swollen index finger, she turned it on—the sudden hum matched Mrs. Maybelline's own. Spittle rested on her lips and a slug of a tongue reached out, absorbed it, and retreated. Her body rocked back and forth in anticipation as the oceanic background appeared and then gave way to diagnostic pop-ups and alerts. Giddy, she clapped her hands together nearly two dozen times in a mere moment. "Now open that new program I uploaded. Hurry up; it's absolutely fabulous!"

Obeying, although somewhat distractedly, Juniper closed the pop-ups and clicked on the newly installed polka-dotted icon. Soon the program "History: Your Way" was blaring a series of horns in announcement of its arrival to the screen. An animated Thomas Jefferson popped into existence and danced about the monitor, from one corner to another, bouncing off the edges, limbs swaying madly, jaw unhinging to produce the words "We the people . . . give you history: your way!"

"See?" Mrs. Maybelline said through her chuckles while nudging Juniper with her sunken elbows. "Fun already. Makes you want to live in the past with him, doesn't it? Fun, fun, fun."

"Fun," Juniper repeated in a monotone. Her mind

was thousands of miles away or, more accurately, in the woods outside her home, which, as of right now, seemed just as far. For what might have been the hundredth time since she and Giles emerged from the underground, Juniper pictured their quiet walk back through the woods that day.

The hole in the tree had closed and Juniper's mind was reeling. "I don't know what to think. Should I have taken a balloon?" she asked Giles. But he wasn't listening. He had pulled the balloon down directly before his eyes. Enthralled, he gazed into it as if it were a crystal ball.

Juniper looked at her friend's face, distorted through the swollen latex. "Giles . . ."

"I can't wait any longer. I want to open it now. Are you ready?" he asked, hands set to untie the string.

Juniper shook her head. "I don't want to watch. Not again." She scanned the woods. "I'll be right over there," she said, pointing to a large tree she could easily hide behind. "Wait until I'm out of sight."

His excitement deflated, but not by much. "Okay, okay."

"Just get it over with," she called out as she made her way to the safe place behind the tree.

He wasted no time.

Juniper heard the scratching pull of the latex, Giles's deep inhalation, and the sudden rush of air screaming down his throat. She covered her ears, then closed her eyes. But regardless of how much pressure she put over her eardrums, she could never drown out her mother's harrowing wail. Even with her eyes sealed tight as could be, nothing but blackness before her, the gruesome visage of her parents succumbing to those balloons still somehow surfaced. There was no escape from it.

And now Giles . . .

A hand grabbed her arm just above the elbow, slightly too hard, and her eyes snapped open. Giles was staring at her, beaming a broad smile. Juniper slowly lowered her hands from her ears. She eyed him suspiciously.

"It . . . it didn't . . . do things to you? To your body?" She saw her father slumped over the dining room table, twitching.

"Of course it did. I feel great!" And he looked great, too, just like her parents had that morning. "I'm not kidding. June, you should have given it a try."

Juniper opened her mouth to tell him that he was

wrong, except she wasn't so sure anymore that he was.

Not long after, Giles left for the day. It wasn't very late, but he gave a hasty good-bye and went racing home at a speed Juniper feared she could no longer match.

"Head out of the clouds," Mrs. Maybelline lectured, directing Juniper's eyes to the computer screen with a pudgy digit, "and back to real life. Just click on the Industrial Revolution icon and it will carry you straight on through it, highlighting all the fun and interesting stuff in no time at all. Then, at the end, there are games for every time period. Isn't that wonderful? Go ahead. Pull it up." Which Juniper did while trying to keep her thoughts from roaming yet again. She was scared of where they'd take her.

"What a great time it was to be an American!" Mrs. Maybelline went on. "You'll feel like you're actually there! By the time you're done, you'll know everything you need to know. I even learned stuff I had no idea about. Who knew what a cotton gin was? Ah, technology. I'm telling you, Juniper, quick and easy! It's the way to go. You won't even feel like you're learning! In the meantime I've got a few phone calls to make and the restroom to use," and off Mrs. Maybelline went, muttering the rest of her errands until Juniper, much to her delight, could not hear them anymore; "e-mail to read, I have to update my mood and status, blog then vlog, check the gossip sites . . ."

Left alone, Juniper clicked the mouse, the screen flashed, and a bright, shiny world of more than a hundred years ago emerged in pixilated perfection. The music mellowed into a peaceful birdsong and the sun shined over a series of pristine factories being built at an alarming pace. Thomas Jefferson walked gaily down the streets explaining this part of America's history in goofy, rhymed stanzas to a bleary-eyed Juniper.

It didn't take long for her to realize "History: Your Way" wasn't fun at all, and it certainly wasn't history her way. She just couldn't relate to what she saw and heard. Everything on the screen left her utterly disconnected. All the details were glossed over, dates and definitions were emphasized more than events and content—there was no how or why—and the games had nothing to do with the lesson. (She couldn't see how a first-person shooter was educational just because you fired a musket.) The program portrayed everybody in town as cheerful drones, and the children brought home shining coins from their jobs and lived in huge, lively houses and the country grew at an astounding rate, covering the land with its new-found technology, bringing peace and love everywhere it spread. Everything on-screen was all so clean and simple and perfect. Toward the end, her animated guide said the Industrial Revolution was what made the country great, but she never really figured out how.

Something, Juniper believed, was missing, and she wanted to know what.

She let the program run its course, taking in what she thought was interesting or important, and, as usual, she decided that when Mrs. Maybelline left for the day she would run down to her father's study, grab a few books on the subject, and educate herself—as well as keep her mind busy and away from her parents, Giles, the tree, and those balloons. She could lose her-self in her books, her spyglasses.

But was this complicating things? Where did it ever get her? Perhaps she should have just accepted what the computer told her. After all, Skeksyl's words still stubbornly lingered in her head. Maybe she really was wasting her time with her books and spyglasses and her pursuit for truth. There were far easier ways to get to the same exact places. The more she thought about it, the more Skeksyl's words took hold.

She never went to the study that day, but she did come upon something else.

After Mrs. Maybelline left, Juniper was making her way back to her room. Passing one of the mansion's numerous bathrooms (there were nine, in fact), she heard her father's voice escaping into the hallway. "I don't understand," he said. He had been known to practice lines in there, and Juniper went to get a closer look. She put her back up against the hallway wall and slid closer until she could see his face reflected in the bathroom mirror. He stared into the looking glass with his mouth gaping wide open, his tongue hanging out and wiggling. His hands prodded about, at times pulling his jaw in opposite directions. He seemed to be attempting to peer down his throat. His head bobbed and weaved, trying for a better view. But of what?

Frustrated, he slammed his hands against the sink and leaned forward, bulging his eyes and spreading the lids with his fingers, one after another. He gazed deeply into each eye, again searching for something. "I don't understand," he said once more. "I don't understand. I don't understand." Then the words quickened. "Idon'tunderstandIdon'tunderstandIdon'tunderstand."

Juniper stepped in front of the door. "Dad? Dad, are you doing lines? You're doing lines, right?"

Mr. Berry turned and looked at her. No, through her—she very well might have been fading away. His hand reached out and slowly closed the door. He didn't say a word.

This is what it has come to, Juniper thought. *Closed doors.*

Then, as if on cue, the front door slammed. The sound typically accompanied Mrs. Berry's arrival, and Juniper ran down the stairs and to the grand hallway to find her mother tossing her jacket on a long wooden bench. "Mom!"

"Not now." Without so much as a glance, Mrs. Berry stuck a hand in Juniper's face and walked on by. Climbing the stairs, she said, "I just talked with my agent. He wants your father and me to star in a film together. The public is clamoring for it. He has a pile of scripts for us to go through. But we have to do this right; the material has to be flawless, stunning. Now, make sure to leave us alone. We can't be bothered."

Tears welling in her eyes, Juniper stared at her mother's back. Her chest began to rise and fall as she desperately tried to think of something to say. "I wrote a screenplay," she called out, finally, with all her heart.

"It's perfect for you and Dad, I know it. Will you look at it?"

Mrs. Berry didn't stop climbing the stairs, didn't even turn around.

Juniper chased after her. "Mom! Mom, please!"

Closing her eyes, Mrs. Berry stood on the top step and brought her hands to her temples. "Juniper . . ." She rocked back and forth. Outside, through an open window, the raven screeched. Mrs. Berry's eyes opened. "Juniper, don't waste our time."

As she watched her mother walk away, Juniper heard Skeksyl's offer repeating over and over within her head, growing louder and louder. She saw her very own balloon waiting to be blown up. She just had to sign her name and breathe.

Without even realizing it, she had crept downstairs, out the back door, and toward the woods. The tree, the raven, and everything they represented were in sight, only steps away.

"You can do this," she whispered. But she knew she couldn't do it alone.

She had to talk to Giles.

She walked to the edge of her yard, the western border. She had never crossed it before, never would have even dreamed of trying lest she be harshly punished and confined even further.

One foot went over, then the other. She stopped. Her parents didn't come out screaming, security didn't rush her, there was no commotion by any of the staff. Nobody cared. And so she kept walking. She walked until she reached her nearest neighbor, nearly a mile away.

A house came into view, another sprawling home much like her own, and along with it came the seemingly obligatory commotion arising from the front yard. Juniper's first thought was that there would be a mass of fans lingering outside these gates as well, seeking autographs and pictures and the like. Her second thought was that maybe she could blend in with them for a little while, experience what it was like. She wanted to see her world from the outside in. Maybe from that perspective things wouldn't appear so bad, maybe everything would make sense. Then she had another, even darker thought, one she never believed she would have. She could just give everything up and walk out those gates as someone else. Maybe she could change the way she acted and looked, change her name and attitude, create a new her, and then everything she was previously would just vanish. Her parents no longer cared; it was obvious she wouldn't be missed. She could start over.

She walked around the house and indeed saw a crowd. But this one was of a different sort. This mob was a bunch of children her age, gathered in a circle. Doing what? *A game*, she thought. *They're playing a game!* And she rushed to join them, no gates to keep her in or out, no parents to call her back.

The circle was tight, so she had to push a bit to get a view of any kind. *This is where a periscope would come in handy*, she realized, regretting she left her World War I replica in her closet. But no, on second thought, had she brought it, such a device would have kept her far from the group. Now she was able to rub elbows with boys and girls who, she imagined, could have been her friends in another life. She was able to listen to their jokes and share in their laughter; she could help spread gossip if so entrusted; she could receive fashion advice. Standing among them, she couldn't believe how wonderful it felt.

Once she squeezed to the front, however, she saw the crowd's main focus: two boys standing in the middle, their fists clenched and held up. An onlooker began chanting and, like a highly infectious disease, it soon caught hold with all the rest. "Fight! Fight! Fight!" Fists pumped in sync, feet stomped the ground, even girls hollered for punches to be thrown. Juniper scanned the circle for Giles, but he was nowhere to be found. She figured that made sense. He wouldn't be anywhere near this crowd.

The fight held no interest to Juniper, and it was over almost immediately after it started. Surprisingly, the bigger of the two boys was on the ground, clutching a bleeding nose.

The smaller boy raised his hands in triumph, and the crowd's chanting shifted to "Giles! Giles! Giles!"

Juniper's head snapped to the center of the circle. She couldn't believe it. The smaller boy was Giles. So badly she wanted to run through the crowd and greet him with a hug, but she looked closer and hesitated. Something was different; she knew it immediately.

Giles was smiling broadly, a toothy grin dominating his oval face. The thick tangles of hair atop his head were gone, shaved clean off, leaving dark stubble and a slight scar behind his ear. His clothes fit him better, his shoes were brilliantly white. In contrast to when they had first met, he now stood ramrod straight, head cocked back and sure. Juniper noticed his deadened eyes—*they're starting to look like my mom's,* she thought, *my dad's.*

In disbelief, Juniper stepped back and hid at the edge of the crowd. She watched as the kids gathered around Giles, congratulating him on his victory. Two girls reached up and rubbed his shaved head. Everyone cheering him on, talking to him—the entire group was made up of the same kids who always tormented him, only now he was their champion, and Giles was loving every second of it.

It worked, Juniper thought. *The balloon gave him what he wanted.* So why wasn't she happy for him? Was she jealous? Did he not need her anymore? Did he have the life he always wanted, everything that she was always denied? It wasn't fair.

Finally, Giles noticed her. She was the only person standing still among a mad rush of jumping and cheering and laughing children. Giles looked at her, then away, then back again. He shot her a quick smile but didn't budge. Juniper made her way over to him.

Giles appeared nervous, perhaps embarrassed. He took a small step back. Then, when she was only a few feet away, he called out, "June, hey!" and pulled her aside, away from the crowd.

"You won't believe it, June," he said in a hushed tone and yet at a hyper pace. "I stood up to him. I didn't let him push me around, and so he challenged me to a fight. I didn't want to, but the whole class followed him here after school."

Juniper crossed her arms. "And that meant you had to fight him?"

"Everything's different now. Did you see what just happened? Nobody's going to bother me anymore." He glanced around to see if anyone was listening. "They're talking to me now. Talking like friends. Girls, too. I won both the push-up and pull-up contests in gym class. I even got picked for football. I belong now. Look at them. Can you believe it? Can you?"

Juniper's face scrunched in bewilderment. "They like you because you hurt someone?"

"Yeah. No. I don't know. I don't care."

He kept glancing over at the crowd. Did he not care about her anymore? Was he friendly with her those few days only because he had no one else?

"Do you ever wonder what you gave up to get like that?" she said defensively.

Giles shrugged. "Just some air. Besides"——he

tapped his torso—"there's plenty more where that came from."

"Aren't you scared of changing, becoming someone else?"

Giles shrugged, waving her question away. "June, come on, everybody changes. What's wrong with that? It's part of life, part of the world. You don't have to be alone." His eyes never left the crowd.

Still, she tried to convince Giles. "I am a part of the world. Just a different part than you. Maybe everyone else was supposed to join us. Ever think of that?" But the words sounded hollow, as if she were trying to convince herself and failed miserably. Juniper wanted to cry. She never thought there was a problem with herself, but maybe there was. Maybe she had it wrong all this time.

Giles started to look annoyed, anxious to get back. Juniper reached out and grabbed his arm. "You'll return down there one day, won't you, beneath the tree. Then you'll go again and again and again."

She was surprised at how easily he shrugged her off. He looked her full in the face, finally.

"June, we can have anything we want. Look at me, I'm fine."

"But . . . but . . . our parents?"

"What about them? They're famous, beloved. Who wouldn't want that? Maybe they're fine, too. Maybe they're more than fine and we were the ones who were changing. Isn't that what growing up is?" Infatuated, Giles glanced back at the crowd, which was now waiting for him. He smiled and slowly turned back to Juniper. "You know, I can hear him now. The raven. I can understand him, like Skeksyl said. I don't know how. It just happened all of a sudden. A voice appears in my head, almost digging away. It overlaps some of my thoughts. Sometimes I don't know which one is me. Isn't that odd?" Giles thought a moment. "But he knows exactly what I'm thinking, what I'm feeling. He told me you'd come here. He doesn't want me talking to you anymore. He says you're just jealous."

"That's . . . that's not true," she muttered.

"I feel stronger, that's all. Just like Skeksyl said I would. He didn't lie."

No, he didn't. He didn't lie to her parents either. They wanted the American dream and he handed it to them in a balloon.

The crowd started calling Giles over. "I . . . I have to go," he said. Abruptly, he turned to leave.

"Giles," she called, stopping him in his tracks. "Is it . . . is it everything you thought it would be?"

He turned to her and looked her in the eye. "It's unbelievable, June. It changes everything."

And that was exactly what she both hoped and feared.

CHAPTER 11

JUNIPER RETURNED TO THE TREE six times over the next three days. Each visit caused her further turmoil. Something was telling her to return to the underworld and make her deal with Skeksyl. And all of a sudden it wasn't the world she was angry with; it was herself. Why did she have to be the way she was? There wasn't any law saying Juniper Berry had to be a lonely girl, forgotten by her parents; she didn't have to be locked away from the world around her. She could do something about it.

The more she thought about it, the more it made sense. If her parents didn't need her, then she should become someone they did need; if they hardly even noticed her anymore, she could become someone they couldn't ignore. Someone they would love. Someone everybody would love. She never had to be alone ever again.

She walked to the tree one more time and placed her hand upon it. Her head dropped and her eyes closed. "I'm scared," she whispered. "I don't know what's right anymore."

Neptune fluttered down from his branch and settled just above her. He knocked his beak against the tree.

Gradually, Juniper's hand crept up to the mark. "Sometimes I feel like the whole world knows something I don't. I just want to belong. Somewhere."

Again, Neptune, his black eyes fixed on Juniper, pecked the tree.

Beneath her finger the mark seemed to burn, aching to be pushed, and Juniper's body filled with this warmth. It felt so comforting. It made the next part simple.

She pressed the mark.

Behind the tree the passageway opened up once more, welcoming her below. Neptune, acting as guide, swooped past her and down into the blackness of the underworld.

Following the raven with her eyes only, Juniper stared into the dark depths in which it vanished. Still, she didn't move.

Why couldn't she take the first step? A new life waited for her at the bottom. What was she waiting for?

A minute later, Neptune returned to the surface, acknowledged her, then flew back down, his screech not fading, not echoing, but deadening.

Then, in place of the flattened cry, drifting out of the darkness came a voice, Skeksyl's voice. *"Juniper."* Her name floated up to her sounding like a dry wind. His voice pulled at her. *"Juniper."*

Her foot touched the first step. She was on her way.

"Juniper . . ."

A second step.

"Juniper."

The voice came from behind her. She whirled around and climbed the two steps back up, just in time.

"Juniper, hello there," Dmitri called to her as he

approached with Betsy slung over a broad shoulder. "Where's Giles?" he asked, driving his ax into the familiar stump, where it angled sharply into the air, forming a sundial of sorts.

Juniper didn't know what to say; she just adjusted her position so that Dmitri couldn't see the opening behind the tree.

Dmitri smiled. "Not around, huh? Are you waiting for him?"

"No . . . I . . . I was just bored." Her eyes drifted back to the stairs; she was surprised to see that they were gone.

Dmitri looked in the direction of the tree as well, his eyes so sharp they could have finished the job his ax started. "You know, Juniper, I envy you. Your world is far different from an adult's. You see things differently. As they ought to be, perhaps. It's easy to lose sight of that. Most of us do. Pressures start coming from all sides and it makes you question everything. You lose sight of what's important."

"What *is* important? Who my parents are? The house we live in?"

"Those things don't make you who you are."

She looked down at her feet. "I guess you're right. I

only have myself to blame for that."

Dmitri was silent for a moment. "I always see you with those binoculars and whatnot, always staring out into the world. What is it you see out there?"

"I see a place that I don't know how to get to. Things I can't touch."

"Don't despair, Juniper. There's far too much of it in the world already. Trust me. People like you are the rare ones. Don't be shaken by what you think you see. It's not the lenses that make you special, it's the eyes behind them. Trust them. They lead to the soul. They haven't led you wrong yet."

Juniper wasn't quite sure what Dmitri was talking about. She felt as if he was keeping something from her. His words filled her with what seemed like wisdom, but nothing concrete. And hardly comforting.

"Well, I should get back to work," Dmitri told her, pulling his ax from the stump. "I hope I won't be in your way over here." He pointed to some nearby trees.

"No. No, of course not," Juniper said with a frown as she turned to make her way back into the house. "I've waited this long," she mumbled to herself. "I can wait a little while longer."

And wait she did. With Kitty at her side, she

watched Dmitri, through her monocular, from her bedroom window, waiting impatiently for his day to end. But he continued to chop away, far longer than usual and never straying far from Neptune's tree. The sun began to set and still he split wood, looking warily over his shoulder every now and then. "Come on, finish," she moaned.

At last the sky began to darken, and Dmitri took his concluding swipes of the day. He slammed Betsy into her usual resting place and walked out of the yard, wiping his brow and eyeing the house. "Finally," Juniper said. She jumped off the bed, ran into the hall . . . and right into her mother.

Unfazed by the blow to her stomach, Mrs. Berry glared down at Juniper, grabbed her arm, and pulled her back into her bedroom.

She tossed Juniper onto her bed. Frightened, Kitty dove under the covers. "Rat," Mrs. Berry spat as she made her way to Juniper's mirror. She walked with a jerking gait, as if being electrocuted. One arm shot downward while the other shoulder shifted violently toward the ceiling. Her head snapped back, her legs buckled, and her fingers tightened into claws. She leaned on the wall for support and caught her breath for nearly a minute. Then, looking up into the mirror, she began stretching the skin on her face, muttering to herself. "I can't . . . I can't take it anymore. What's happened to me? Lines . . . my face is covered in lines . . . there's one, there's another . . . oh, these bags beneath my eyes . . . my lips, I think they're getting smaller. Dear God, I'm hideous." Horrified, she continued poking and prodding at her face, pulling at her hair, making odd faces and grunts. Juniper didn't understand; *She's beautiful,* she thought.

Mrs. Berry turned to her daughter and a look of confusion crossed her face. "Ju . . . Ju . . . Ju . . ."

"Juniper. My name's Juniper." She was nearly in tears. It was as if her heart went as flat as paper, or deflated like a balloon. Her mother had left their love behind, all their memories. And now even her name was gone, too.

"Yes, I knew that. Juniper. Yes, of course. Juniper, dear, do me a favor."

"Yes?" Juniper clasped her hands together.

"Don't ever get old," her mother went on. "Prevent it any way you can. Or at least get a very reputable plastic surgeon."

"But I don't see anything wrong."

"That's because you're just a child. You think it's easy to carry a career into your later years? Much must be sacrificed."

Juniper wondered just how much her mother already had sacrificed. To her, it seemed like nearly everything.

"There's talk I won't be nominated this year. Can you believe it? That last movie, they're saying I wasn't . . . I wasn't . . . Oh, it's just absurd; it was the director's fault. Moron. I can fix it, though. On this new movie . . . I can start fresh. I know I can. I've done it before." Mrs. Berry appeared to be recalling something. "I keep asking him to help make me beautiful again, but it never seems to last anymore."

"Who? Who do you ask?" Juniper knew, of course, but she didn't receive an answer to this question. Instead her mother continued to ramble on.

"Tastes change. Trends. Looks. The people . . . they're never satisfied. It's never enough. Never. This next film will mean everything. But I don't know how much further we can go. I . . . I think there's something living in my mind. Something's moved in when I wasn't looking . . ."

She continued ranting about youth and beauty,

aging and withering. At one point she stood before Juniper's mirror and pulled her mouth wide open, stuck out her tongue, and peered down it just like Juniper's father had done days earlier. She yanked on her eyelids, tugged at her hair, poked at her teeth in constant search of something. Right before Juniper's eyes, her mother vanished. Indeed, like she said, it was as if her body and mind had been overrun, hijacked. She had hardly any control of it anymore.

Mrs. Berry slammed her hands down on the vanity. "This isn't fair!" she screamed. "I don't know who I am anymore! I'm not me! I'm not me! I'm blank!" She reached down and grabbed her calf. Her nails dug in deeply, and then she scratched all the way up. When she pulled her hand away, it dripped bright blood. Her mad eyes followed each flowing drop to the floor. "Is this me? Is this even mine?" She grabbed Juniper by the shoulders, staining them red. "Tell me!"

Terrified, Juniper broke free and ran from the room and downstairs, her heart beating rapidly. Kitty ran right after her.

She found her father in his study. He was sitting at his desk, his back to her and the door. She could only see the top of his head and bits of his arms and legs, but she could tell he was trembling. His arm dropped to his side and, like his wife, blood dripped down his fingers and onto the carpet. He mumbled, "There's not going to be much left. I'm vanishing."

"Dad?"

He turned around, tugging his sleeves past his wrists. Drowsily, he glanced at her, then back at a picture on his desk. He picked up the frame, streaking the glass with blood, and studied the image. Finally, he nodded. "Juniper. That's right." He held it up to her. "I wrote your name on this picture so I don't forget. I've been so forgetful lately."

"What are you doing? What's going on?"

"I'm working."

"No you're not."

"I'm trying to," he said. "I hit the wall again."

"Dad, you're bleeding!"

"No, no, no. It's nothing." He pointed to his script. "The words don't mean anything to me anymore." With the blood on his finger he drew a sad face at the bottom of the page.

"Then why don't you stop?" Juniper begged. "Take time off. You've done so many movies, everyone loves you, you don't ever need to act again."

"Don't you understand? Acting is all I have."

"What about me? What about Mom? Our family?" Juniper pleaded.

Once more he glanced at the picture as he shook his head. "Juniper, come now. What am I without my characters? Take them away and there's nothing of me left. I have to keep going. I have to keep the film running. It's my heartbeat."

"Heartbeat? Dad, what about us?"

Her father stared at her blankly. Juniper hardly recognized him anymore. And it was at this moment that she saw most clearly.

"I thought I wanted to be like you. But I'm not. If I ever do become a writer, I won't care if anybody picks up my books. I won't care if no one knows who I am."

"Then how will you know you're alive?"

"The same way I know you're not!" Anger filled her, confusion and pity and disgust, and she fled the room.

"That's not what the world thinks!" he screamed after her. "They love me! They love me, you silly girl! Long after I'm gone, they'll still love me!" He paused. "They have to! Or what's the point? Girl! Silly girl! Get me my wife! We have to talk, you silly little girl!"

And talk her parents did, for that night Juniper watched them make their way across the lawn and to the tree, greeted by the screech of Neptune. She gathered her coat.

This time Juniper would follow them all the way down.

CHAPTER 12

J UNIPER CREPT ACROSS THE YARD, eyes locked on her parents. She thought for a moment about calling Giles, even as she knew she couldn't. She didn't know if she could trust him anymore, and besides, there was no time. But this didn't keep her from wishing he was by her side.

Her parents descended behind the tree, Neptune joining them, sitting obediently on Mr. Berry's shoulder, the two in the midst of a conversation, like two old friends. Then they were out of view.

By the time she reached the tree, the opening was still there and she quickly and quietly made her way down the stairs in pursuit of her parents. The trek down felt like mere seconds.

Juniper reached the bottom and gazed the length of the hall, but there was no sign of anyone. She knew her parents were most likely already seated at the table, eager to receive their balloons.

Slowly, she crept closer. When her parents' voices became clear, she crouched down, leaning against a closed door with markings of a giant tree with branches reaching out, grabbing at stars, and listened to the conversation taking place.

"The intervals are becoming shorter," she heard Skeksyl say. Then he let loose an absurd giggle. "I thought you said you were done."

"Don't mock us. Just let us have it." It was her mother. There was panic in her voice, desperation.

"Of course. Of course. More of the same?"

"You know what we want. Stop playing games," Mr. Berry demanded.

"You must understand, I want to stretch this out. I don't know how much more you two have to offer. This may be our last meeting."

Juniper didn't like the sound of that.

"What are you talking about? We still have air to

breathe. You'll continue getting what you want. I don't see what good those balloons do you anyway."

"I assure you, Mrs. Berry, I get just as much from my balloons as you do from yours. That's why I'll be so sad to see you go." But then, oddly enough, he laughed. It didn't make much sense to Juniper. Not much did anymore.

"Let's get this done with. Give me the quill," Mr. Berry said.

"How are your arms, my friend? I assume this ordeal is taking its toll on you, and you're, no doubt, still fighting it. It won't help. You know this. Just give in to it. Let your body be. Revel in your success and everything that comes with it."

"It doesn't feel as good as I thought it would," he responded.

"But here you are."

"Yes, here I am. Now fill up that balloon."

"As you—" There was a pause. "One moment."

Juniper heard a chair scrape the ground. Her parents were whispering, and the torch flames whipped as if caught in a light wind. *What's going on?*

Thump . . . thump . . . thump . . . Skeksyl's staff. A sliver of shadow reached the hall. The shuffling of his bare feet quickened. There wasn't much time. He was coming for her.

Fearful and trembling, Juniper pushed open the door she hid against and entered the room, shutting it quickly but softly behind her. She held her breath and heard Skeksyl's muffled footsteps outside, the muted pounding of his staff. A full minute passed, Skeksyl pacing the hall, Juniper completely still.

And then nothing. She exhaled, finally turning around to figure out where she was.

In the room was a very old man chained to a table. He was dressed in a black suit, with a long gray beard ending somewhere near the middle of his chest. Framing his blue eyes were the strangest goggles Juniper had ever seen. The lenses moved on their own, whirling and spinning by several cogs and gears. Kept in place with thick leather straps, the contraption was made of brass and looked very heavy. Juniper would have loved to try them on.

On the table to the left of the old man was a small machine that he was in the process of cranking. The machine consisted of various twists of steel and billowing steam. There was a funnel at one end and a long tray at the other, and as the crank turned, the entire machine quaked and whistled. In the old man's right hand was a sharp metal stick of some kind, a silver needle that he used to prod inside the crevices of the contraption. It looked like tough work, and the man had taken off his jacket and hung it on the chair behind him.

A fedora was tucked beneath the table, and every few seconds it jumped as if something was trapped beneath it. To the old man's right, filling half of the room, was a tree with absurdly long branches stretching from wall to wall. Growing from this tree were wires, blue and red and white wires—at least they looked like wires. They each had a life of their own, the thin, stringlike cables wrapping around the branches, twisting in the air like hanging snakes, writhing in such a way they appeared to dance or blow in a breeze. Every once in a while the ends of two different wires met and ignited a spark. The spark then fell to the ground and sizzled, leaving a very small indentation in the earthen floor. Something too small for Juniper to identify crawled out, something that buzzed and glowed. From the hole, it ran to the tree, up the trunk and branches, until it reached the ceiling, where it then dug a hole into which it finally disappeared, going who knows where. It was a very strange room.

Juniper, however, could not concentrate on all of this, only seeing it from the corners of her eyes in pieces, for the startled old man was her main focus, just as she became his.

"Oh dear," he said. "You shouldn't be here. You are in great danger. He must not find you."

"Who . . . who are you?" Juniper asked, her back to the closed door, amazed to find such a man living in such a place.

The old man sat back in his chair, pausing from his work. With ancient hands, he removed his goggles and rubbed his weary eyes. "I . . . I don't remember," he answered.

"You forgot your name?"

"There's no use for it anymore." He stroked his beard in a contemplative manner. "You can give me a name, if you'd like."

Instantly, the name jumped into her head. "Theodore."

"Theodore, then. My name's Theodore. What is yours?"

"Juniper. Juniper Berry."

"That is a lovely name."

"Why are you chained to that desk?" she asked,

pointing to the thick shackle wrapped around his left ankle and bolted to an iron ring in the floor.

"He keeps me here. He keeps me working."

"On what?"

"His balloons. I make them."

"Skeksyl needs you to do that?"

"These are very special balloons. Making them requires great care. A single balloon takes weeks to produce. But you are in luck. I am just finishing one now."

He slipped the goggles back on, returned his hand to the crank, and rotated it. He continued to poke the machine with the needle at random intervals, eliciting a shower of sparks, some of which settled into his beard and sizzled and smoked. Juniper took a cautious step back.

Soon enough a red balloon emerged from within the revolving gears and onto the tray. Theodore reached into his suit jacket and removed a pair of brown leather gloves and put them on. Then he picked up the balloon, inspecting it closely, the lenses on his goggles switching out, seemingly at random.

Finally, he tossed it on the table and grunted. "It's flawed."

"Flawed?"

"I must have made a mistake somewhere along the way. It happens. It's a very intricate process." He looked sad. "It's his favorite color, too. Would have been part of his personal collection, for those most special of exchanges. But, alas, this one is nothing but a normal balloon." He brought it close to his mouth, blew on it, and shook it. When he was done he handed it over to Juniper. "Here, it's yours. It's worthless to him, ordinary. To you, though . . . perhaps you can find some use for it." Then he winked at her. Or was it his goggles?

With a tiny smile she thanked him and placed the red balloon in her pocket. "What are they supposed to be?" she asked. "The ones that come out right, what do they actually do?"

Theodore sat back, folding his hands. "Tell me, young Ms. Berry, what are you doing in such a place as this?"

"I . . . I followed my parents here."

"Oh. I'm very sorry to hear that. Did they just discover this place? Sometimes I can hear a commotion outside my door, but what goes on out there is a mystery to me."

"I think they've been coming here a long time."

"I see." He leaned forward, his eyes large. "You must listen to me closely. You must stop them. You must not let them come back here. Not ever again."

"Why? What will happen?"

"I'm sure you've been noticing it already. They must be changing right before your very eyes, you poor child. They no longer resemble the parents you remember, do they?"

Sadly, Juniper shook her head.

"And do you know why? Do you know what your parents lose in their exchanges?"

"They blow up a balloon."

"Remember, these are special balloons. They work quite differently from the ones you are used to. No, these balloons do not take air."

This scared her. "Then, what?"

"They take their souls."

Juniper's face dropped into her hands.

"You knew this, didn't you, deep down? You saw the signs."

Through her hands, she cried, "Yes."

"Juniper, they cannot, must not, fill any more balloons for him."

"Why? Why does he do this?"

"My dear girl, he feasts on them. With his sly methods and silver tongue, he collects as many as he can, storing them so that they can ripen. Then, when he finally inhales one, he gains decades of life. He has stored dozens of them and inhaled dozens more. He is trying to live forever. This is no creature to be trifled with. He is older than you can possibly imagine, and he will be here longer than any of us will ever manage." He paused, his body deflating to match his balloon. "Except for me, perhaps. He forces me to feed on them as well."

"Who is he?"

"*What* is he is more like it. He is a black mirror, a dark thief, banished here a long time ago."

"Banished from where?"

"From a place no girl like you belongs. A place you shouldn't even think about lest you go mad. Trust me, Juniper, when I say there are worlds much worse than this. Now, please, you must help your parents."

"What can I do?"

"Don't let your parents return here. Stop them at all costs. Before it's too late."

"But it *is* too late. I want my old parents back."

"It's impossible, dear. You would have to get to all those balloons he has safely locked away, and even I don't know where he keeps them. And besides, he'll never let you pass into the hallway beyond. He's always there. Hold on to the parents you have."

Juniper ran up to the table. "Please. There has to be a way."

"Juniper, you must be careful. He'll want your soul most of all. A child's soul, especially from a child like you, is worth far more than any adult's. It's just so rare that a child is willing to barter for it."

"I have to help them."

"No. Impossible. And now you must leave. He knows a balloon was due today. He'll be here soon."

Juniper looked around the room. "I can help you leave this place."

"Child, I can never leave. My destiny is here." Then he smiled. "At least I have a name again."

Juniper smiled, too, weakly. "Theodore."

"Theodore. Now go. Be wise. Be safe, young Juniper Berry. And remember, sometimes that which seems ordinary is really most extraordinary of all."

She opened the door and, finding the hallway empty,

tiptoed out, making her way toward the entrance. She only glanced back once and, to her surprise, she saw another couple heading toward Skeksỳl. Juniper didn't stare long, though; she broke into a run, up the stairs, and back to the mansion.

CHAPTER 13

THE HOUSE WAS DARK. The house was silent. The house was still. Not a single bulb glowing, no banter of any kind, no footsteps, no rustling of papers, nothing. The house was beyond sleep, nearly dead. Juniper needed to find her parents, and yet the thought alone terrified her.

"Mom?" Her voice cracked with fear as she entered through the back door. "Dad?" But, as expected, there was no response. Her heart began to beat rapidly; she clenched her hands together to keep them from shaking in a similar rhythm. She had to find her parents before they consumed their balloons.

Slowly, she walked to the dining room, where she'd seen them after returning the first time. Kitty was most likely back in Juniper's room, hiding in her bed. Juniper wished she could trade places. Sometimes being human was unbearable. But she pushed on.

Eyes closed, she rounded the corner. The dining room was steps away. This was it.

She didn't want to look. *Please*, she said to herself, *don't let them be in here. Don't let them be in here.* Forcefully, she opened her eyes.

Her parents weren't there. The room was empty, not a sign of their presence. Juniper sighed in relief.

Perhaps there was still time. Gaining confidence, she searched the entire first floor, finding nothing. Her parents had to be upstairs.

Grabbing the rail and holding tight, she made her way to the second floor and straight to her parents' bedroom, the wood floor creaking beneath her steps. At night those noises were always loudest. At night nearly every sound was ominous.

With a deep breath, she pushed the door slowly.

There they were. Facing each other at a small table before an oversize window overlooking the grounds, the moon pinned to the sky and wrapped in clouds, they sat motionless. Mr. and Mrs. Berry's heads were tilted all the way back so that their wide eyes stared at the ceiling, their mouths hanging open, bodies stretched out, arms dropped at their sides. And below their chairs, just out of reach of their open hands, were two deflated balloons.

"Mom? Dad?"

There was no response from her parents, but the closer she came the more she believed she could hear something. She was sure of it. The sound was faint, below even a whisper, but now, only feet away, she was positive the muffled sounds were escaping from her parents' mouths as if something were stuffed down their throats. She took another step closer. Then one more.

Finally, when she was no more than an arm's length away, she saw her father's throat twitching in the moonlight. His neck throbbed like a hyper pulse. The noise intensified. It was a slight gurgling sound and becoming something more. He was trying to say something.

"Dad?" Slowly, she reached out her hand to touch him. His skin was cold, and when she tried to prop him up, he would not budge; his body was rigid. In his mouth, his bulbous tongue shifted and some bubbles bubbled forth and burst. "What is it, Dad?" she asked.

She brought her head forward, turning it so that her ear was near his mouth. "What is it?"

Then, weakly, the words trickled free and found her. "Help us."

Juniper's eyes widened.

There was a loud crash as her mother fell forward onto the table and began writhing. Her knees thrashed into the base, knocking a glass to the floor and shattering it. Her arms flailed wildly; her face slammed repeatedly onto the table, drawing blood from the bridge of her nose. She had absolutely no control of her body.

At the same time, across the table, Mr. Berry joined his wife in her contortions. Shaking convulsively as if electrocuted, he slid from his chair and fell face-first to the floor, where he floundered like a swatted fly.

Juniper stepped away, horrified and helpless. Tears welled up in her eyes. "Mom! Dad!"

In an instant, everything went still. At the sound of

her voice, her parents' bodies went limp and the house fell silent yet again. But only briefly.

Mr. Berry's face was scrunched against the floor, mouth open, with blank eyes staring out at Juniper, when something popped in his throat. His eyes flickered and two words soared from his mouth in a primal scream: "Save uuuusssssssss!" Then again: "Save uuuussssssss! Save uuuussssssssss!" Over and over and over again.

Juniper slammed her hands against her ears and tore out of the room. She flew down the stairs and out the back door, into the yard, the words enveloping her like fog. Her thoughts were a tangled mess of fear, panic, and terrible, terrible grief. Consumed with herself, she had delayed in helping them for far too long and now her parents were possibly lost for good. Her feet kicked madly beneath her. She tried to outrun everything that was happening; she wanted to run so hard that she ended up in the past, back when her life was normal. She ran and ran and ran, refusing to stop until she was where she needed to be.

Until she found Giles.

She soon reached the outskirts of Giles's property,

stopping short when she saw figures on the lawn.

Under pale moonlight, Giles knelt in the grass. Lying facedown on either side of him was a man and a woman.

"Giles!" Juniper called. She dived to the ground and hugged him tight, but he didn't move; he didn't even look at her. She heard him softly crying.

"They ... . they won't move," he stammered. "Their eyes were open and their mouths, and they were making noises and shaking and I had to turn them over, I couldn't take it anymore." He pointed to two deflated balloons discarded by their sides. "They couldn't even wait until they entered the house, just like I couldn't. And now ..." He trailed off, sniffling. "And for what? What's left of them now?"

"I know," she said. "My parents, too."

Giles finally looked up at her and nodded sadly. Then it was his turn to hug her. Their bodies filled with warmth, the love of a friend. "I have to tell you something," he said as he pulled away. "These aren't my parents. Not my real parents, anyway. They're Mr. and Mrs. Abernathy. I . . . I don't have any parents, not anymore. I used to live with my grandmother in their servants' quarters, before she passed away. I had only worked for the Abernathys, but they took me in, cared for me, at least until . . ." He stared at the two figures on the ground. "I didn't want you to know."

"It doesn't change anything, Giles."

"They treated me nice once, like a son. But that was a long time ago, when they were different people."

"I saw them," Juniper said. "Not even an hour ago. I followed my parents down, and they came soon after."

"This could have been me," he said in a haze. "I started to feel it, the changes. Just that, it's so little, like almost nothing you would really notice. It feels like I forgot something but couldn't even imagine what it was, or if it was important. I didn't think anything of it. I thought I'd only do it a few more times, before it got really bad."

"Giles, you never needed to change anything."

"But I always felt like I had to. If you went to school with me, you wouldn't like me either. I know it. You would have joined all the rest. You don't know what it's like. You're a pretty girl. That changes things. It means you don't talk to me and you giggle with your friends while glancing in my direction. You like the boys who beat me up. If we went to school together, I'd want you to like me. But you wouldn't."

"I like you now. I like everything about you. School wouldn't change that. Nothing would. I'll always be the one to decide who I talk to, and I want to talk to you. The Giles I first met."

Giles locked eyes with her. "You . . . you mean that?"

"I do. I really like you. I missed you so much these past few days."

"You promise you won't change your mind?"

"I know who I am."

"You won't forget about me? Really?"

"Never."

Without hesitating, she moved in and hugged him once again. She put everything into that hug, all her love and pain and sorrow and confusion, and she felt all his as well. Then, with his eyes firmly closed, Giles sighed. "Thank you."

They separated, and Juniper looked at the Abernathys sprawled on the lawn; she thought of her parents, and her anger surged. "Skeksyl's not going to win, Giles. We're going to end this and make things right."

"What . . . what can we do?"

She stared hard at him. "We're going to get those balloons back."

CHAPTER 14

AFTER MOVING THE ABERNATHYS safely into the
house, they made their way back through the woods.
On the way, Juniper told Giles all about Theodore and
the balloons and what exactly they stole. They knew
it wouldn't be easy, but they had to somehow get past
Skeksyl, find out where that hall beyond his table led,
and hope they could find the balloons. It wasn't much
of a plan, but it was all they had.

It was a damp and dreary night, and any search for
stars would prove fruitless, as the sky was nothing but
a cloud of fog. The tree, however, was in sight, and
Juniper's and Giles's futures, as well as their parents',

were in grave question. Their stomachs churned with dreadful anticipation. Above them, the raven was perched ominously upon its usual bough, head bobbing side to side in sadistic glee. As was always the case, all other birds kept clear.

Juniper found the mark on the tree and the stairway opened up. "Ready?" she asked.

"No."

Juniper smiled for a moment, then fixed him with a look. "I'm not ready either, but those balloons aren't going to just float up here themselves." She took a step forward, then stopped. She looked back at Giles. "I'm glad you're with me," she told him. "I couldn't do this without you."

He gave her a shy smile and said, "Me neither."

With that, Juniper and Giles placed their feet on the cracked steps and journeyed back down beneath the tree, Neptune gliding past them to guide the way they were all too familiar with. Unfortunately for Giles, the raven squawked a barrage of words that assaulted his ears.

"The words are stronger down here," he told Juniper as they descended the stairs. "It's telling me to convince you to take a balloon this time. It's practically begging. He wants you."

"They want us both," Juniper said. "Just like they took my parents and the Abernathys. We can't give in to Skeksyl's temptations. No matter what."

They made their way down the steps and hall and past the six carved doors and found Skeksyl waiting for them at the table, the two chairs already in place, as if all were normal and expected.

"Ah, my friends," he squealed, his two hands meeting at the fingertips. "I was hoping to see you again. Please. Please, have a seat." Without rising, he offered them the two empty chairs with a swipe of his hand and a slight bow of his hooded head.

Once seated, Juniper spoke up. "I . . . I couldn't wait any longer."

"Yesssss." He stretched the word, again his yellow smile shining through the cloaked darkness. "Precious time has been lost already, dear girl. But . . ." He stared at the writhing shadows on the wall. "You're not here about the writing business, are you? No. Not this time. It's something else now. Yes, I'm sure of it. There are no secrets between us, Juniper Berry. Your parents aren't well, are they?"

Juniper froze in her seat. She was not expecting this.

Giles, too, stared blankly at the gaunt figure across the table.

"I know what has happened to them, Juniper. They can't be saved. It is much too late for them. They will be lost to you, dead, without my help. But there is hope, Juniper, and I can give it to you. I can give you the power, the knowledge, to save your parents, bring them back from the void, even rekindle the love you have been denied all this time."

Juniper and Giles were rooted to their seats in shock. But Skeksyl wasn't finished. "And not just that. I'll make a special deal with you. I'll give you everything. For just one balloon, I'll give you everything you ever dreamed. It's wisdom, Juniper. You seek wisdom, enlightenment; the world defined and explained. A voice to tell you what is what. Why are you the way you are, what has happened to your parents, and what can you do about it? You want the answers in your lap because with them you will know how to fit in, how to belong. But, most of all, you will know how you can finally have your family back."

"Yes." The word escaped before she could stop it. Was she really considering this? The more she thought about the offer, the more her feelings morphed into genuine yearning. And the more she admitted it, the more the yearnings burrowed into her heart.

How were they to get past Skeksyl, anyway? It was impossible. But saving her parents, herself—that was something she could do, right here, right now. With such a gift she would never be lost again. She would know true happiness.

"I can give it to you. Easily. Your very own cheat sheet to the world. No more running to your books, no more running to your spyglasses or Giles or even to me. You'll never have to seek answers ever again, for you will see the reasons in everything. I'll give you the world, Juniper, in black and white. You'll have your parents back, and nothing will ever trouble or scare you again. You want to feel like you belong some-where? And save your parents, no? This is the only way."

"Please." Suddenly she couldn't have such a gift soon enough. Skeksyl understood. He always had. And as much as Juniper feared his terrible power, she knew there was no other way. She had come down here to save her parents, herself. And now she could. For just one balloon.

Skeksyl reached into his cloak. "Tell me, Juniper,

what is your favorite color?"

"Yellow," she answered.

And out from Skeksyl's cloak came a yellow balloon, which he placed directly before him, and a red balloon, which he placed before Juniper. "Red is mine," he said, to which Juniper replied, "I know." His head tilted at a slight angle upon hearing these two small words, as if he didn't understand them. But he was eager and shrugged them off. Then, from within his cloak, he procured a quill and immediately wrote the word "wisdom" on the yellow balloon. Fervently, he brought the latex to his mouth and blew it to size. "The stuff of dreams," he told her as he attached the string, sealing in whatever it was he breathed into it.

Finally, grinning, he handed the quill over to Juniper. "Your turn."

With her hand quite still, she grabbed the quill, marveling at how comfortable it felt in her hands. *One balloon*, she thought. *Like Giles. I'll only do it this once, then never again. I won't become like my parents. One balloon and everything will be right again.*

The quill touched the balloon, creating a small black dot.

Across the table, Giles called out to her. "Juniper..."

She raised the quill.

"Quiet, boy. Let her finish," Skeksyl snapped, refusing to take his eyes off Juniper. "We'll get to you soon enough. Go ahead," Skeksyl told her. "Sign your name."

Juniper set the quill back to the latex, concentrating on her parents.

Giles interrupted yet again. "Juniper, wait."

She knew he was attempting to stop her, to remind her of why they came, but she couldn't budge.

"Boy, you will get your turn," Skeksyl said with a voice of ice. "Sign your name, Juniper, and the deal will be done. Your parents will be filled with life; they will love you again. Sign your name. Do it." He grew impatient, like Juniper had never seen him before. He was on the edge of his seat, leaning far over the table. "Do it!"

The quill began to tremble in her hand.

"Sign your name!"

The ink flowed as the quill moved elliptically upon the red balloon, forming a jagged *J*.

Giles stood. "Juniper, don't!" He took two steps toward her before Skeksyl's staff shot out and blocked his path.

Neptune screeched as Skeksyl rose to his feet, sending his chair flying out from behind him. In an instant he was looming menacingly over Giles, seizing him by the throat. His pale fingers nearly overlapped around Giles's slight neck. "That strength getting to your head, boy?" He lifted Giles several feet off the ground and slammed him against the wall. "Perhaps it's time you knew real strength."

Juniper could only watch, the quill now frozen in her hand.

Giles kicked and gagged and turned blue, and Skeksyl laughed. "Look how pathetic you are. And now Juniper will sign her name and finally see you as you truly are."

But Juniper disagreed. She already knew exactly who Giles was. He was her friend, the best a girl could ever have.

"Tell me, boy," Skeksyl went on, seething, "what could a pathetic wretch like you possibly offer someone like her? You are still so very weak. Useless flesh and nothing more."

"Ju . . . June . . ." Giles choked.

Juniper looked at her friend struggling in Skeksyl's grasp, barely breathing, and something shifted inside her. Giles was fighting for her, and knowing this, she no longer cared for the answers Skeksyl offered. The weak boy filled her with a strength she never knew she had.

Quickly, with Skeksyl's attention diverted, Juniper reached into her pocket and found the balloon Theodore had given her. She smoothly swapped it with the one on the table. *I'll find my own answers*, she thought. *I like them better.*

And she made the switch just in time. Skeksyl tossed Giles to the floor, and his head shot back around to her just as her hand returned to the quill. "Enough!" he shouted. "Sign your name!"

As Giles slowly recovered on the floor, Juniper put the quill to the ordinary balloon and signed her name in full. Skeksyl grinned and giggled madly. "That's it. Good girl. Now finish it."

Juniper brought the balloon to her lips and blew it to its fullest, her eyes never leaving Skeksyl. Even though his face was shrouded in its usual shadows, she could feel how greedily he watched her. He had been waiting for this moment, aching for it.

Skeksyl snatched the balloon away from her before she could even seal it with a string. "Yours will taste best of all," he hissed. A sharp tongue darted out of his mouth, licking his pale and cracked lips. His hands, like the rest of his body, were trembling violently. He had to set one on the table before moving on. His breathing became rapid, strained. Odd noises and squeals escaped uncontrollably. His smile grew and grew.

Finally, urgently, he opened the balloon, brought it to his salivating mouth, and inhaled its contents.

Juniper and Giles watched with utmost horror and tension as he greedily engulfed her breaths. The air rushed from the balloon, shrinking it in seconds. Skeksyl's neck pulsed with Juniper's sweet air. He savored every breath.

When the balloon was completely deflated, he sat back in his chair, smiling wickedly. His body went limp. The balloon slipped from his fingers and fell to the floor. "You fill me warmly," he told her. "It feels like nothing I ever experienced. So pure. So true."

The room fell silent. Juniper's mind raced. She was out of options.

Suddenly Skeksyl's body shot forward. He became rigid. His hands, stiff and clawlike, grasped at his neck. "What . . . what did you do?" He gagged and retched, yellow mucus flying from his mouth and sizzling on the wood table. Beneath the cloak, his body bubbled. His staff dropped at his side as he fell to his knees.

Alarmed, Neptune flew around the room, screeching like Juniper had never heard, as his master doubled over in severe pain.

"Now!" Juniper yelled. Giles ran from the room and down the dark, forbidden hallway. But before she joined him, Juniper took her yellow balloon with the word "wisdom" written on it, held it before Skeksyl's shadowed face, and popped it.

CHAPTER 15

JUNIPER CAUGHT UP TO GILES AMID THE SHADOWS of the hall. "June, you did it! You switched balloons! How'd you know that would happen?" he asked her.

"I didn't," she responded. "But he had to be using specially made balloons for a reason, right?"

"For a minute there, I thought you were going to sign your name on the one he needed."

"For a minute there, so did I."

They hurried down the hall, not knowing what they would find or where the balloons would be stored, but Juniper felt more alive than she had been in a long time. She nearly floated through that suffocating darkness.

If Giles could see her, he'd see her smiling.

The hall seemed to go on for a very long time—the dark tends to have such an effect on the senses. Juniper couldn't help but wonder what part of the world sat above them and what was going on there. Maybe one day she'd walk that very spot, the Earth stretched out before her, the horrors below long forgotten. There was so much waiting up there for her. But she first had to safely escape and save her parents.

When she and Giles finally emerged from the hall, what they saw was astonishing.

Before them was an underground world, so large and so vast. There was a multitude of torch-lit hallways shooting off in various directions from the immense cavern they stood within. There were staircases twisting and turning overhead, leading to gaps in the ceiling of the cave and to who knew where. Everything seemed to stretch for miles with no end in sight, a subterranean labyrinth of immense proportions.

"What do we do?" Giles cried, his voice echoing like the loudest thunder. "Where do we go? He'll be coming for us soon!"

"I don't know! I don't know! The balloons can be

anywhere!" She felt the panic rising up inside her. They only had one shot at this and if they failed . . . no, she couldn't think about that. Her hands slapped at her thighs in frustration, and that was when she felt it. Her monocular. Quickly, she pulled it free, extended it, and brought it to her eye.

She traced the underworld, looking for some type of sign, a clue to set them on the right path. But each hall led to a staircase or another hall or a dead end; some stretched so far they could have been endless. Throughout, there were doors with markings on them similar to the one she entered to find Theodore. If they were to try each hall, each door, they could spend a lifetime searching for the balloons. It seemed utterly hopeless.

Then, through the lens, Juniper's eye came upon something.

In the middle of one long hall, the floor was aglow, and, in this light, the ground actually appeared to be moving. Every other hall she peered down was identical to the next, one after the other, all but this one.

This had to mean something. It was their only shot. And so they ran toward it.

The glow intensified with each step, and when they

reached it, they discovered the floor was made up of a continuous stream of sparks, similar to the ones in Theodore's room. They were all running beneath the same carved door.

The image on the door consisted of hundreds of flies circling and settling on a thin crown with roses blooming within its center. It made no sense to Juniper, and she had no time to ponder its oblique meaning. That would have to be left for another day. For now, she just had to get inside and hope the balloons were there.

"We can't waste any more time," Giles said.

He reached out with the tip of his sneaker and was about to step down on the sparks when Juniper suddenly stopped him. "No," she said. "We shouldn't block their path."

Giles looked down at the sparks. "Block their path?"

"They seem alive, don't they?"

"They're sparks," Giles pointed out.

Juniper bent down and pulled out her magnifying glass. Inspecting them closely, she saw they were the tiniest of black-eyed creatures, almost human in appearance, with small wings rubbing together and creating a glow.

"Amazing," Juniper whispered. "Just amazing."

"Why are they all going in there?"

But Juniper didn't respond. She reached out her hand, gently cupping it, and several of the sparks crawled into her palm. "They tickle. They don't burn at all."

"June, your hand's glowing."

She looked at it and indeed it was. The glow slowly stretched up her arm, and she was filled with tremendous warmth. "They're beautiful," she said, "magical. What are they doing in a place like this?"

Soon enough, after a gentle buzzing, the stream of sparks ended and the hallway was left bare. She returned the sparks she held to the ground and they, too, disappeared beneath the door.

"Hurry," Juniper said, rising to her feet. "Let's see where they lead."

Giles stepped in front and, with ease, swung open the heavy door.

Inside, at the center of the room, was yet another tree. This one glowed white, a thousand sparks covering nearly every inch, moving about, buzzing with great intensity. There, tied to each branch, were dozens of balloons, all different sizes, with sparks running up their strings.

Juniper looked on in awe. "It's like Theodore said. The souls inside the balloons are ripening. That's why some are bigger than others. They must have been here longer. The sparks must be caring for them."

As Giles reached for the nearest balloon, the attached sparks scattered. He pulled it down and examined it, only to see a name he didn't recognize written across its face. "How am I going to find mine?"

The fact was, he didn't have to. His balloon found him. On a midlevel branch, one balloon was pulling itself down toward him. Giles inspected its red face and found his signature written in dark ink. "There you are," he whispered. Gently, he untied the string from the branch and gazed past the surface of the balloon, looking for something inside, a part of himself, perhaps. "It felt good to be strong," he said, more to himself than Juniper. "I'm going to miss it." He paused a moment, then undid the knot and reclaimed his soul. His body seemed to shine brighter than the room, and the sparks buzzed with excitement.

"Help me untie them," Juniper said.

"There're too many. It's going to take us forever to find our parents' balloons."

"No, we have to free them all," Juniper said. "Each one."

Hurriedly, they untied the balloons, one by one, gathering fistfuls of strings in each hand. Any more and the two friends might have floated to the ceiling. The sparks quieted with the removal of each balloon and, with nothing left to ripen, fled the tree.

Once every balloon was untied and the tree was left completely bare, Juniper and Giles turned to leave. Except their exit was blocked by a wall of sparks.

Juniper, unsure how to proceed, addressed them. "Please, I'm sorry. We have to do this. There are people in great need." She stepped toward them and the sparks pulsed with movement. Shifting her balloons into one hand, she stuck out her free hand to touch them as she did before, to move them, ease her fingers through their glowing wall.

This time, however, there was a terrific burn, as if she had placed her hand directly into a blue flame. Quickly, she yanked her hand free and shook it cool. The pain immediately faded.

"Please," she cried. "I have to save my family."

A lone spark left the wall and traveled up her body. This one didn't hurt, not at all; it felt like the ones outside the door, pulsing with warmth. The spark crawled up her neck and settled on the rim of her ear. Inside her head, she heard a lovely, almost angelic voice. "We can't let you leave with those balloons," it said. "You must trust us. It's for your own safety."

"But . . . but . . . I don't understand."

"We know you have a good heart. Upon touch, we can tell such things instantly. That is why we must stop you. If every single balloon is taken from this room, such an act will unleash them."

"Unleash them?" Juniper's voice cracked.

"His legion, his slaves, will come for you. They will fill these halls in seconds. They won't let you escape."

"Please, we have to try."

"We are trying to save you. Take whatever balloons you need, but leave the others. As long as there is still a balloon on the tree, you will be spared."

Juniper considered this compromise. She could just take hers and Giles's parents and retie the rest to the tree. That was what she had come for, was it not? But in her mind she saw another girl like herself, another

boy like Giles, and how they suffered the same fates. It wasn't fair. Leaving a single balloon behind, she wouldn't be able to live with herself. "I can't," she told the spark. "We have to take them all. Every last one."

"And why is that? Do you know all these people?"

"No."

"And yet you would risk your own lives for them, knowing full well that there will always be more balloons, more sacrifices?"

"Yes. Yes, we would."

"I see. Very well. It is rare for us to come upon someone like you down here. Your light glows brighter than all of ours put together. We will do our best to delay the beasts. You must hurry, though. Pray they never reach you. Good luck."

"Thank you."

The spark left her ear and joined the others. Together, each glowing creature rose to the ceiling and vanished. Juniper turned to Giles. "Let's get out of here."

They ran from the room with balloons in tow like colorful clouds, strings pulled tight into the palms of their hands, back in the direction they had come. Juniper expected to see Skeksyl leading an army of ghouls at any moment, and if that was to happen, she wasn't sure what she and Giles would do. She glanced back, to the sides, into the distance, but there was no sign of anything. Perhaps the sparks could hold the beasts at bay.

Yet there was no time for relief, however momentary. They raced down the hall, pulling the balloons away from the ceiling lest they pop. To Juniper, they seemed to act as a parachute blowing behind her, slowing her down. Her arms ached immediately. Running like this, they were such easy prey.

They made their way into the massive cavern from which all points led, and it was there that they heard the noise.

Throughout the cave, down all the halls, each and every door was swinging open.

"They're coming for us!" Giles shouted.

For an instant, Juniper saw things emerge, things she couldn't identify but that chilled her to the core. Grotesqueries on two legs. It turned her voice into a desperate wail. "Run! Run faster!"

The strangest, most hideous noises grew behind them, a mélange of nightmares, but she and Giles refused to glance back. The forbidden hallway leading back to the staircase and to their homes was just ahead.

Entering it, they wished for light. The darkness was complete; anything could be in there waiting for them. Juniper expected to run right smack into one of the monstrosities pursuing her, but still she bravely pushed forward, the balloons bouncing together behind her, sounding like an absurd orchestra.

The tunnel stretched and stretched, and moments later, overwrought with fear, Giles tripped and fell to the ground. "The balloons!" he screamed. He had let them go and they were immediately consumed by the darkness. "I'm sorry," Giles uttered. "I'm sorry, I'm sorry, I'm sorry."

Juniper heard the anguish in his voice, but there was no time to lose. "Hurry, we have to get them."

They could feel the strings dangling across their faces like spiderwebs. Frantically, they grabbed what they could, swiping through the black air like blind men. All around them, the noises grew. "We have to go!" Giles yelled.

"There might be some left," Juniper cried.

And just then, there was light. The sparks sat in the ceiling, revealing the few remaining balloons. Tears in her eyes, Juniper thanked them again and retrieved the last dangling strings. The lights dimmed out, then took off down the hall while Juniper and Giles continued in the opposite direction.

Perhaps, Juniper thought, *Skeksyl's still at the table, frozen. Maybe we can run right by him, far past whatever's behind us, and he'll never bother us again.* But when they came out of the darkness and into the room, Skeksyl was nowhere to be seen.

"He's looking for us!" Giles called. "Go faster! We're almost there!"

They ran down the hallway, the stairs getting closer and closer, the noises falling farther and farther behind them, and that was when Juniper came to a screeching halt. Silent, she stared at one of the carved doors.

"What are you doing?" Giles called. "Why are you stopping?"

In a panicked hush, she replied, "I have to rescue Theodore."

"June, we have no time. We have to get out of here. He'll catch us. Our parents, the rest of the people in the balloons, they'll be lost."

"Giles," she said softly, "I have to do this. I have

to try. No one deserves to be trapped in a place like this."

He looked at her with warmth, with admiration. His eyes calmed, but when he spoke, it was with urgency. "We can't let anyone ever come down here again, can we?" he said. "Not ever. We have to make sure we're the last." He looked back to the stairway. "We have to end this."

Juniper knew what he was thinking, and it made her want to hug him and never let go. "I won't be far behind," she said. "A minute. That's all."

"What if you need me?"

"You have to get started. We're near the end now." She put her shoulder against the carved door and pushed. Giles called out to her, but she pulled the balloons gently through the opening and walked inside.

The moment she stepped into the room, thousands of sparks flew past her, into the hall and toward the noises of the beasts.

At the table, dressed in the same suit with his hat still sitting and randomly jumping beneath the table on the floor, Theodore looked up from his work. "Juniper. What's going on?" He saw the balloons filling the room in two big bursts. "Are those . . . ? Did you . . . ?"

Juniper nodded.

"No, no, no. This is foolish. You must get to safety."

"I've come for you."

But Theodore didn't budge. He pointed to the shackles. "These chains will not break, whatever you do." He gave them a sharp tug as if to prove the point. "Did you find a use for that balloon I gave you?"

Again, Juniper nodded.

"You are a brave girl indeed. The world needs people like you. That is why you must leave. Now."

"There has to be a way to get you free."

"These chains open for no key. They were created by dark hands, by something we couldn't possibly understand. Perhaps one day a smart girl like yourself will figure it out. But, I assure you, I cannot be saved today."

"But—"

"No. Juniper. He'll find you. They'll find you. You must run. You must escape now."

"Theodore, I—"

"Now!"

Just then the door swung open, and in the frame

stood a hobbled Skeksyl. His body was even more grotesque now, his skin riddled with boils and lumps. "My balloons!" he screamed.

Juniper backed toward the tree, terrified to the core. The balloons knocked precariously against the branches, making their sad music. If he came at her, they might tangle around the tree limbs, they might pop.

"You could have gotten away like your weak friend. The one who pathetically abandoned you. But you had to come back. And for what? Him?" He pointed a blistered finger at Theodore. "You are playing with destinies far greater than your own, girl. Now give me my balloons." He reached out for her, to finish her, and that was when Theodore reached for his hat.

From beneath it came dozens of flying sparks. They shot across the room and toward the tree in an arc of light. In unison, they latched on to Skeksyl's leg. He let out a nightmarish wail as his flesh burned. The room filled with smoke and stink as he smashed whatever sparks he could.

"Go!" Theodore called out to Juniper. "Run!"

Juniper gave him one last look and the old man nodded. "It's okay," he said. "It's okay."

Still grasping the balloons, with Skeksyl writhing in pain beneath the tree, crushing sparks to death in his fists, she opened the door, squeezed through with her rescued souls, and ran for the stairway. It was so close now.

From behind her she could hear the screech of Neptune in pursuit. She didn't even need to glance back to see how far off he was. Wings flapping frenetically, the raven was upon her in no time at all.

But, strangely, it didn't strike at her. She couldn't even see it. Where did it go?

Then she heard the noise. *Pop!*

Juniper swung her arms wildly at the bird, but it was too high for her to reach. *Pop! Pop! Pop!* it pecked, and three more souls were lost.

She bunched all the strings into one hand and once again reached into her pocket. Desperate, she grabbed the monocular and extended it with a quick snap of her wrist. Then, gripping it like a club, she swung.

She connected solidly; there was a crunch, and the raven flew all the way down the hall like a batted ball, landing limply in Skeksyl's hands.

His leg sizzled and steamed. It was destroyed. He leaned against his staff for support, staring at the dead bird in his mutilated hands.

For what seemed like minutes, nobody moved. Juniper was almost sure her heartbeat was audible. It filled her ears with its throbs. She placed a hand to her chest. It was then she realized the noise was coming from somewhere else, somewhere above her. Inside, she smiled. Giles.

Skeksyl dropped Neptune to the floor. In a shattered voice of delirious pain and limitless anger, he spoke. "Those are my balloons. My souls. And I want them back! I! Want! Them! Back!" He came for her. He limped, far faster than Juniper had thought possible. "You're miiiinnnnee!" he howled.

At first she couldn't move. The sight stunned her in its horror. He filled the hall with his frightening figure. He was on the hunt; the ghoul wanted blood.

Juniper turned and began to race up the stairs. But the space was small and the balloons slowed her greatly as they cluttered against the ceiling. She could hear the wounded Skeksyl gaining on her, panting and grunting. It was impossible to look back, for the balloons blocked her view, but she swore she could feel something swiping at her ankles.

The noise from above, from the outside, continued

and grew louder. She was getting closer.

"There's no escape, Juniper!" Skeksyl yelled, and the words might as well have been screamed directly into her ear. He would have her in his clutches in mere seconds. The end was near.

Juniper climbed on, her muscles burning. Tears filled her eyes but she refused to let them fall. *Be strong,* she thought. *Be brave.*

Then, finally, she saw light. The night was over. The sun had begun to rise.

"Giles!" she called.

"June! Hurry!" he yelled back.

His voice filled her with hope. She pushed on. She climbed higher and higher. Just a few more steps, just a few more and . . .

She was out; she made it, the sunlight beaming down upon her in powerful bursts. To her right, balloons were tied to a tree. To her left was Giles and, incredibly, in his hands was Betsy. Not only did he lift it with ease, the tree was nearly chopped down. It was almost over.

But that was when she felt the hand grab her ankle. She fell onto her back.

"Mine!" she heard from beneath the tree. "I'm

going to keep you alive forever, Juniper! I'm going to keep you alive so that you can wish for death!"

"No!" Giles screamed, dropping the ax and racing over. He grabbed Juniper by the wrists and began to pull. But he made no difference. Skeksyl pulled them both closer.

"Giles! The balloons!" she yelled. "Save the balloons!"

Quickly, Giles grabbed the two sets and ran to a nearby tree. His hands blurred with speed as he tied them securely to a branch.

Juniper tried to break free from Skeksyl's grip but it wouldn't give. He had her. He pulled her closer still.

She tried to plant her feet, but it was no use. Her hands clawed helplessly at the dirt.

Closer to the hole she came, closer to him. He pulled her all the way back to the ice-cold steps.

Giles dashed for her, arms outstretched.

"No! Finish the tree!" Juniper called.

Torn, Giles hesitated.

"It's our only chance!" she screamed.

With amazing strength and speed, Giles picked up the ax and chopped furiously at the twisted trunk.

One swipe, two swipes, three . . . Soon the tree began to creak.

Juniper's mind raced. *If it falls with me down there . . .* but she pushed the thought away. She had to.

"Yes! Yes! Come to me, Juniper! You're mine!"

Juniper looked back and, in the faint light, she could see Skeksyl. More than that, however, she could see his face. His hood was down and she saw him fully for the first time. It was the most disturbing and sickening image she would see for the rest of her life. It wasn't even a face. It was the remains of a face, the remains of a man, one with no soul of his own.

Still, she glared directly at him. "I'm not going anywhere. Not any part of me." And with her free leg she kicked him as hard as she could right between what were supposed to be his eyes. His head snapped far back and she fell backward, free.

Giles struck the tree one more time and the loudest crack of all echoed. Skeksyl looked up just in time to see the tree come falling down upon him.

The hole was covered in a mass of debris and, with the tree no longer standing, the stairway collapsed, each step crumbling and dissolving as if it had never existed at all. With an inhuman wail, Skeksyl was lost beneath the shifting earth. His arm, still grasping for Juniper's ankle, breaking ground like an oversize root, was all that was left. Then that, too, vanished, disintegrating into dust and carried away by a strong wind.

It was over.

CHAPTER 16

Morning had come, and sunshine struck the balloons in magnificent blasts. The dust from the fallen tree rose up and danced in the yellow rays pulsing through the overhead leaves. Bouncing together in the breeze, the balloons were a bubbling wind chime eliciting a welcome sense of peace. They sat aglow among the branches, as if the sparks were tending them still. Below them, eyes closed, Juniper and Giles embraced for some time. They didn't say anything; they didn't need to.

When they finally came apart, they knew there was one final step they had to take, the most important step, the most terrifying step, because, if it didn't work, their families would be gone for good. All would have been for naught.

They went through the balloons one by one, searching for their parents' signatures. Juniper came across one, her mother's, and weighed it in her hands. The balloon felt like nothing, like a handful of fog. She handled it delicately, caressing the orange latex. It seemed even more vulnerable now. Only the thinnest of layers kept her mother's soul from mixing with the morning air. Juniper gently tied the balloon to her wrist for safekeeping. Beneath the orange shell was precious cargo indeed.

In the end, there were twenty balloons in all—five for each parent. If there had been more, they were now long gone.

Giles and Juniper nodded at each other, and then he turned and ran for home, the ten balloons trailing behind him, rainbow drops against a blue sky. Juniper looked up to her parents' bedroom window. She took a deep breath and hoped it wasn't too late.

She entered the house to find Kitty waiting for her. Yipping, her dog jumped as high as her chest. "I'm okay, I'm okay," Juniper said, calming Kitty. "But we need to hurry." As she stared at her feline dog, her voice cracked: "It's going to work, isn't it? It has to." Kitty released a soft whine and rubbed against her leg. "I hope so, too. Here goes everything." Together, they made their way to her parents' bedroom.

Juniper pushed the door open. Inside, her father was still sprawled on the floor, while her mother remained collapsed awkwardly against the table. Their eyes were open and blank. The sun burst through the immense windows, illuminating the broken bodies.

Falling to her knees, Juniper undid one of the balloons and, hands trembling, placed it to her father's lips. It reminded her of when she was a child and her parents lovingly fed her with a spoon they flew through the air like a plane. Now, much too soon, it was her turn to care for them. She emptied the balloon's contents down her father's throat, making sure not a single breath escaped. Then she did the same for her mother.

Finished, she stood back, waiting for something to happen. Only nothing did. Her parents were completely still.

"No, no, no. Please," she cried. Desperate, she shook them, slapped their chests, kissed them. Still nothing.

With the fear of forever losing her parents taking strong hold of her emotions, she quickly undid a second balloon each and squeezed the air back into their lungs. "Come on," she begged. "Come on. Work."

Anxiously, she waited for the souls to settle. Her parents had to come back to her; they just had to. Face wet with tears, she gazed at them, wishing them back into existence. "I need you. I need you both so much."

Just then, there was a flicker in their eyes, a twitch of life in their hands and legs. They uttered soft moans as if waking up from a long sleep riddled with nightmares.

More balloons. Juniper sprang to her feet and grabbed two more. Kitty watched closely as the third and fourth balloons were carefully issued back to Mr. and Mrs. Berry.

Impatient and achingly nervous, Juniper repeatedly slammed her palms against her thighs. "Hurry. Work. Help them," she pleaded. "Help them." She grabbed Kitty for comfort, squeezing her tight.

With tear-filled eyes, clutching Kitty close to her chest, she watched as life flowed back into her parents. She saw their skin glow, their chests heave. Their once-vacant eyes suddenly reflected a previously forgotten past. Slowly, they both sat up, shaking their heads clear of a powerful daze.

Still groggy, her parents settled their eyes on Juniper. For some time they stared at her, unable to speak.

Please, let it work, Juniper silently hoped. *Please be my mom and dad again.*

More silence. Then . . .

"Juniper? Juniper? Oh, thank goodness! Juniper!" Mrs. Berry leaped forward and grabbed her daughter, hugging her as tightly as she could. She planted kisses all across her face, refusing to stop even as the excitable Kitty barked and nipped at their legs.

"My girl!" Mr. Berry cried as he joined them. "You did it! Oh, my little girl, you did it!"

It was the moment Juniper had waited so long for. It was the same hopeful thought that had pushed her through this nightmare, the image she wished for each night as she went to bed. They were back. Her parents were finally back.

Once Mr. and Mrs. Berry calmed down—they couldn't stop kissing each other, couldn't stop kissing Juniper, even Kitty—Juniper went on to explain everything that had happened since she first spied them entering the underworld beneath the tree. She told them about Giles and Dmitri and Skeksyl and Neptune. She told them about the black room of dreams, about Theodore and the sparks and the chopping down of the tree. She told them how she missed them so very much.

Then, most important of all, she told them that she had the last of their balloons, one more each. They could reclaim the contents as well, but they all knew this meant they would have to give up everything they had gained in their deals with Skeksyl.

"I don't know if you'll be able to accomplish so easily everything you once did," she told them. "There are no guarantees. Dad, I don't know if your characters' voices will come."

Mr. Berry grabbed her hand. "The words will come. Only they'll be mine now, no one else's. It may not be what everyone wants, but that's okay. I'll be doing what feels right to me, and I'll have you and your mother. That's what I should have known from the beginning."

"We were so lost," Mrs. Berry said. "We had everything, and yet, nothing. This is what matters most, the three of us like this. We've missed out on so much. You missed out on so much, Juniper. We're so, so sorry." She looked at her husband, then back at Juniper. "Sweetheart, get us those balloons."

The balloons were happily returned, and Mr. and Mrs. Berry were whole once more.

"What's the first thing you want to do, Juniper?" her father asked, grinning a forgotten grin, his complete self for the first time in ages. He put her face in his hands, caressing her cheeks with his thumbs, wiping away her tears. "Anything you want. What shall we do?"

Juniper didn't have to think. "I want to have a party."

Mr. Berry laughed and pulled her close. "A party it is!" And he kissed her on her forehead.

Mrs. Berry grabbed Juniper and twirled her in her arms, a long-delayed dance. Mr. Berry joined the embrace and Juniper closed her eyes.

"My beautiful family," Mrs. Berry said. "We're back together. Everything is right again."

Juniper couldn't agree more.

EPILOGUE

WHEN THE DAY OF THE PARTY ARRIVED, so did nearly fifty guests. Juniper, however, did not know any of them. She found their names on the balloons and, with the help of her parents' various employees, spread word across the Internet, hoping the owners would take notice and come to reclaim what they had lost.

Juniper had never been so happy.

Nor had Giles. At nearly the same time as Juniper's parents reclaimed their balloons, the Abernathys reclaimed theirs. They rejoiced as well, embracing Giles as the son they never had. Life as it ought to be returned.

It wasn't so for everybody. Not every person came to the party. Some may never have come across the invitation, for some it might have been too late—as it almost was for the Berrys—while others may have had no desire to give up the lives they had gained in losing a part of themselves.

In the backyard, the balloons were everywhere, and Juniper was thrilled to see those who were eager to find theirs and open them like birthday gifts. Smiles spread seamlessly from face to face as tears of joy fell. There were happy reunions left and right, and people sang and played games and lived as if they were children again.

At one point, as she and Giles returned to reflect on the ruins of the tree, she was tapped on the shoulder. "I'd like mine back, too." It was Dmitri.

Juniper looked up at him. "I thought I might find your name on one of the balloons. You knew what was happening all along."

Dmitri nodded. "When I first came here, I made a deal with that . . . that thing. He can be . . . persuasive. And when I inhaled that balloon, I felt different. I began to hate myself and I vowed never to return there.

But there was still the temptation, always the temptation, and that was why I tried to chop it down. Your father stopped me, of course, and I'm glad he did."

"But why?" Giles asked.

"There will always be temptation, wherever we go in life, with whatever we do. There will always be an easier way out. But there's nothing to gain from that. We have to overcome such urges; we have to be stronger. I fought hard and I won. Every day, I stared down that tree and everything it represented. But you two are something else. You didn't fight for yourselves, you fought for others. That makes you two the strongest people I know." He laid a hand on Giles's shoulder, then found his balloon tethered to a nearby tree. "Now, if you'll excuse me, I've been waiting for this a long time." And off he went, undoing the string.

Juniper turned to Giles. "You hear that? There are different kinds of strength."

Giles smiled and grabbed Juniper's hand. Together they walked through the party, witnesses to the beauty of life restored.

Throughout the day, Juniper talked to nearly everyone. Her parents proudly paraded her around, introducing her to anybody who would listen. And not once did she wish she was somewhere else, not once did she yearn for that which she didn't have, not once did she wish she was something she wasn't. She looked each person in the eye and said, "Hello. I'm Juniper Berry."